LOVE'S
Mended
Wings

*Effie begins to blossom in the
light of the hard-won love of
her aunt.*

LOVE'S
Mended
Wings

Effie begins to blossom in the light of the hard-won love of her aunt.

LaJoyce Martin

Love's Mended Wings

by LaJoyce Martin

©1987 Word Aflame® Press
Hazelwood, MO 63042-2299
Printing History: 1989, 1991, 1994, 1996, 2000

Cover Design by Paul Povolni

Illustrated by Art Kirchhoff

All Scripture quotations in this book are from the King James Version of the Bible unless otherwise identified.

Printed in United States of America.

WORD AFLAME® PRESS
8855 DUNN ROAD
HAZELWOOD, MO 63042-2299

Library of Congress Cataloging-in-Publication Data

Martin, LaJoyce, 1937—
    Love's mended wings.

    (Pioneer trilogy ; bk. 2)
    I. Title.   II. Series: Martin, LaJoyce, 1937—
Pioneer trilogy ; bk. 2.
PS3563.A72486L6   1987   813'.54   86-33955
ISBN 9-932581-10-2
ISBN 0-932581-09-9 (pbk.)

To
Karen Rose
my daughter-in-law

Contents

Foreword

As we grow older, our heritage grows dearer.

Brazos Point and The Springs, the geographical setting of my second fiction book, is the land of my nativity. The tiny town of The Springs in Bosque County, today called Walnut Springs, retains an aura of mystery. At the turn of the century it boasted a thriving college, the Central Texas railroad shops, numerous churches, two doctors, and a main street choked with prosperous businesses.

Predictions as to its future ran rampant. With plenty of water, a pleasing climate and ideal location, prognosticators said it would soon outpopulate Fort Worth and Dallas.

But, alas, it was not destined to be so. The college eventually closed its doors, the railroad shops burned to the ground, and the doctors moved on to more remunerative territory.

Today, Main Street is lined with empty, delapidated buildings. The Lion's Den, a meeting place for senior citizens, provides the social breath of the centenarian.

The great revival meeting in the thirties spawned many dynamic ministers. A small church of elderly pilgrims remains, pastored by Brother William Lamb. The congregation includes retired ministers, who have returned after a lifetime spent in the King's employ. My own parents, Reverend and Mrs. Donald Berry, have returned "home."

Those of us who have our roots in The Springs are selfishly grateful that our little city never reached the heights of modern commercialism. We like to return to the peaceful solitude of valleys that knot into unexpected hills, of bubbling Steele Creek, and of spreading walnut and pecan trees in childhood's "city park" with its ancient gazebo and spring-fed fountain.

Dear birthplace, this is as you should be and doubtless shall remain, unspoiled, tranquil, flanked with memories as beautiful and as well-kept as your cemeteries.

LaJoyce Martin

Chapter 1

Surprising News

" *T*aint fair! You looked in th' post yesterd'y! T'day is my. . ." Dessie wasted words on the unheeding ears of William, who sped toward the house on winged feet, clutching the treasure.

"Mama! Joseph got a letter!"

"Lay it there on th' mantle till Joseph gets in from spring plantin'."

"Ain't you gonna open it up 'n see if'n it's important er not?"

"We don't open other people's readin', William. 'Tain't p'light."

"Is it p'light to look 'n see who writ it?"

"If'n th' letter is backed with a return name, wouldn't be no hurt in it."

"Then who does it say?" William held the letter up for Martha to see. "I can't read nuthin' but printin'."

"Ask Effie. She's th' most learned o' th' bunch." Martha favored Effie with a proud smile.

"I-it's from J-Jim C-Collins," Effie said.

Still chafed, Dessie flounced through the open front door, along with a yellow wasp. She shed her books and stockings in one quick shucking session, while Martha worried the indignant wasp on through the house and out the back door with her tattered cup towel. "Well, who was th' post for?"

"Joseph."

"Oh, wow! Mayhap he's got him a bonnie!"

William made a wry face. "What a disgustin' thang to say, Dessie. A bonnie! Who'd want a bonnie nohow?"

"I seen you douse Nellie Gibson's pigtail in th' inkwell."

William interrupted lest Martha hear and reach for the razor strap. "Joseph's letter ain't from no *girl*!"

"How d'ya know?"

"Effie read th' backin'. It's from Jim."

"That's next best."

"That's *first* best," corrected William dourly.

"Wish Joseph'd hurry so we can see what th' message is."

Martha heard the comment. " 'Tain't becomin' fer young lasses to be so nosy, Dessie," she disapproved.

Dessie waited impatiently for Joseph's return from the field, intercepting him at the wash basin.

Joseph reached for the lye soap lying on the hindmost weathered board of the crude table that served as a wash stand, which was unpainted and gray with wear. He splashed the water from the granite foot tub onto his face, arms and hands, generously applying the nondescript-shaped cake of cleanser to his tawny skin.

Shaking the excess water from his eyes, he buried his face in the clean, bleached and blued flour-sack towel that Martha had hung on the wooden peg for him, turning it dingy with the residue of grime. Fresh field dirt hid safely underneath his fingernails and refused to be ousted. Henry waited for the once-white towel, staining it worse.

"Joseph! Joseph! You got a letter!" Unable to suppress the tidings any longer, Dessie's eyes danced with excitement.

"Me?"

"Yep. It's from Jim. Wonder what news it bodes?"

"Just letting us know he's still alive probably. It's about time I'm hearing from that old roadrunner!"

Thirteen-year-old Dessie followed Joseph through the open back door into the kitchen, chattering nonstop. A pot of soup, smelling of potatoes and onions, sat simmering on the back burner of the black wood cookstove, while the delicious odor of freshly baked gingerbread strove for recognition amid the potpourri of smells.

The long harvest table with its matching side benches staged a happy family reunion each evening. The "President's Boys"—Chester, Alan, and Arthur—sat along with William at the backside of the table, while Henry sat in a cane-bottom chair at the head to say grace. Matthew, Joseph, Dessie, and Effie sat on the front, and Sally pattycaked in her highchair. Martha "waited the table," a family tradition of her upbringing.

Supper was a time of sharing, planning, deciding. Life's drawing board was brought out at mealtime and the future's blueprints were discussed.

Joseph put his letter in his pocket, honoring his

mother's hot meal above the herald of a friend.

"Ain't you gonna read it, Joseph?" prodded Dessie, after Henry said grace.

"Not until I get enough strength," laughed Joseph. "Mama's cooking is better than any old letter!"

Martha reached for Joseph's tin cup and refilled it with cold, creamy milk, then stepped to the stove to remove the gingerbread from the warming oven. It was a comfortable old kitchen with grease-splattered wallpaper tacked to the plank walls. A needlepoint print above the table that said "God Bless This House" had hung there for as long as Joseph could remember. The past six months had been especially blessed.

"We got the spring crops laid in, Mama," Joseph said.

Martha glanced down at her firstborn son, seeing past his dusty, patched overalls and thatch of ungroomed hair. He sat erect and handsome, with clean, rugged features and firm muscles. *Joseph's th' kind o' boy that'd do any mother proud,* she thought.

"I talked to th' teacher t'day 'bout gettin' Effie in school come fall," Martha broached the subject foremost in her mind.

"That's good, Martha. I was hopin' you would," Henry looked up from his steaming bowl, holding a pone of cornbread in midair. He always pursued a matter if he felt it discussion-worthy. "Miss Vivian is gonna take 'er, ain't she?"

"She said she would if'n she stayed on teachin'. She's thinkin' on quittin' on 'count o' her age an' health."

"What? You mean Miss Vivian won't be our teacher no more?" Chester's piqued voice rose in a wail.

"Mayhap an' mayhap not," Martha said in her chil-

14

dren-are-to-be-seen-and-not-heard tone. "She's nighin' on seventy."

"We may be hard put to find a replacement," Henry supplied. "Teachers er hard to come by. 'Specially good 'uns like Miss Vivian. Big demand fer 'um. People er gettin' more education-minded. An' th' big schools always get th' best 'uns."

"I jest hope whomsoever we get will take Effie," Martha shared her concern with a heavy sigh. "That's th' most important thang."

With the subject exhausted and dessert devoured, Joseph pushed back his bowl. "And now, if you'll all excuse me, I'll read my delinquent letter from Jim."

He opened the letter with maddening slowness and read to himself. A hush fell over the table and Dessie tried to read Joseph's facial expressions to determine the letter's tenor, finding a swing from frowns to smiles, which told her nothing.

"Is it good news er bad?" she goaded, forgetting Martha's admonition.

"Dessie!" Martha reproached. "Hoe yer own row an' let ever'body else hoe their'n."

"Well, I jest. . ."

"It's some of both." Joseph methodically folded the letter back into its original shape before answering Dessie's question. "Jim lost his only sister, and he has been detained in the West trying to settle up her affairs. She didn't have but the one little crippled girl who preceded her in death. Jim's taking it real hard."

"She lived in th' Territory?"

"A place called Santa Fe, west of Caprock. Jim says it's a beautiful place."

15

"When'll he be comin' back our way then?" Henry wanted to know.

"Well, that's questionable," Joseph took a deep breath, akin to a sigh. "He's planning to get married!"

"*Jim*? Get *married*?"

"It is hard to imagine," admitted Joseph. "He often teased me about the coach house keeper's daughter at Caprock. Charlotte Browning was her name. But when I turned the tables on him, he'd say a stage driver had no business being in love—that a driver had no call to marry until he was ready to throw down the reins and stay put. 'I never met a woman I loved better than driving,' he used to say."

"Musta got bit right hard," Henry chortled. "Do ya know th' woman what stole his heart?"

"He didn't mention her name, but I'm sure I don't. He never spoke much about any woman except his sister. I knew he'd never marry as long as this widowed sister lived; he felt an obligation to her."

"Didn't waste no time after she departed though, did he?"

"No sir, he didn't."

"Musta been a whirlwind courtship."

"I'm sure he was lonely after he lost his sister, but a hurried up sort of wedding is out of character with Jim. I can't put it all together."

"He never mentioned nobody he was sweet on?"

"Not a hint."

"Do you think he'll keep drivin' his coach after makin' that kind o' statement?"

"Now that's another surprise. He wants me to take the line."

16

"He *what?*" Martha jumped.

"Wants me to take his route, coach and all."

"But Joseph! Coach drivin' is terrible dangerous!"

"You mean like runaway horses or broken axles?"

"No. Indians!"

"Indians are more likely to attack the prairie schooners for supplies. Or sometimes they consider them a threat to their buffalo. They learned two decades ago that a stagecoach isn't a potential danger to them; there're very few Indian holdups anymore."

Martha's drawn brows showed she was unconvinced, but Henry deftly changed the subject. "Where do ya think Jim will live?"

"His sister's property in Santa Fe fell to him. A nice house already furnished and a good deal of land. There're no other living heirs. He'll live there, I'm sure."

"Aw, we'll miss Jim! He won't be comin' when he gets a wife. Why does he have to go an' get married?" the outspoken Dessie grumbled.

Joseph shook his head. "Beats me! He didn't ask my permission!"

"Then you will consider takin' th' route?" Henry knew the answer before he asked.

"I'll give it some serious thought, Papa. It's something I've always wanted to try my hand at. Jim's coming through in about a month. Wants to show me the route, explain the baggage rules—and he asked me to stand up with him at his wedding."

"Where's th' weddin' to take place, Joseph?"

"He didn't say. Fact to business, he didn't go into detail at all about his change of lifestyle. . .leaving me with a lot of unanswered questions!"

17

"But drivin' a stage still seems dangerous an' you so young" Martha tried again to object.

"We'll have to trust God, Martha," Henry reminded, suggesting finality to the subject. "Joseph's of age."

"How old is Jim anyway, Joseph?" Dessie asked. "He was my favorite bachelor."

"Probably not much past thirty," Joseph answered. "Been driving since he was real young. Inherited the stage from his father. He brought you to us, Effie, on one of his early runs. That's been ten years ago!"

"I w-was o-only th-three."

"Did Jim say anything else?" Dessie loathed missing out on anything.

"He said to tell everyone hello, especially Effie, and that he wants Effie to come to see him in the wild, wild West!"

"Never!" Martha avowed, but Effie laughed gleefully.

"She'd be safe enough," promised Joseph. "When I'm making a freight haul sometime, I can take her and bring her back."

"Y-yes!" beamed Effie, ever ready for adventure. "To s-see my b-birthplace!"

"If I am to become employed, Papa," Joseph said thoughtfully, sidetracking any further arguments from Martha, "that means you and I have a special project to finish before I leave."

"What's that, Joseph?" asked Martha.

"We're going to build Effie a room of her own before I budge an inch. I sha'n't leave until I see my little sister well situated. Do you think we can get it staked off tomorrow, Papa?"

Henry nodded. "When th' table is cleared, we'll draw

18

up th' plans."

"I'm glad th' spring crops is laid by," Martha said. "Now if'n we can jest get some rain, Henry."

But no rain came.

Chapter 2

Joseph's Confession

When Jim Collins walked into the Caprock Stage-stop in the Territory, Charlotte Browning handed him his mail. The scrawled handwriting was unmistakably Joseph's. He had just yesterday posted Joseph a letter; the letters crossed en route.

He tore the envelope open eagerly. He read:

Dear Jim

You rascal! Where have you been keeping yourself? We've not seen mustache or beard of you since last October. Must I remind you that the winter snows melted two months past? Have you forgotten us?

"Memories are like reading a book the second time," you once told me. "You're busy getting the plot the first time, but the second time around you

21

discover the little details you overlooked." I couldn't sleep tonight for remembering some of those details. Time has done little to erode some flint-etched memories.

Even now I can feel my bur-dodging feet picking their way across the sunbaked trail to our front door ten years ago, bearing the letter from Uncle Charles informing us that he was bringing his motherless child to live with us.

Did the change take place in me when the letter arrived or when Uncle Charles left Effie and headed west in search of gold, never to return? In retrospect, I think that a single sentence from my beloved uncle cast the mantle of manhood about my shoulders. It seemed that while others my age still capered about in immaturity's short trousers, I climbed into the long, scratchy britches of adult responsibility. My carefree boyhood days ended with that one sentence: "Take care of my angel." I felt an awesome burden fall upon me.

Nothing can erase the mental picture of Mother's face when she saw the small, gnarled body of Effie. Her awkward gasp, together with the worry-lines on Uncle Charles's tired face as he struggled with inadequate peacemaking efforts are not a pleasant reflection. Mother didn't mean to be cruel; it was her upbringing, her lack of education.

I labeled the next decade the "Ten Years of Tribulation," an apt description indeed, though my own trials could not possibly have compared to Effie's.

"The child has evil spirits!" Mother hurled at

Papa, who found himself caught between her bitterness and his own sympathy for his younger brother's unfortunate baby. Mother was ashamed to take Effie anywhere—even to church—and hid her from society's curious stares.

I tried my best to make a pleasant life for Effie. Oh, how I tried! But Mother's rejection sometimes outweighed my best intentions. As I look back now, I am sure Effie could not possibly have survived without her departed mother's Bible, left behind by Uncle Charles. I have never seen such dogged determination as the child put forth to learn to read Aunt Rebecca's "Book."

And to complicate matters, there was the deacon's wife who loved nothing better than to turn life brown around the edges with her poison tongue. Leave it to her to start a wicked scandal about Effie's origin! Even the parson came dangerously close to losing his position when he tried to defend the morals of the Harris family.

My own efforts to teach Effie to walk and talk brought great rewards. At first, my purpose was to surprise Uncle Charles when he returned (not knowing that he would not be returning).

Looking backward, the ten years seem like a fast-moving drama for the whole family parading across the screen of my mind. The scene brightened for me when I met up with you and began my plans for a trip to The Territory to visit the place of Effie's birth and Rebecca's death. Good and bad intermingled. My sister, Sarah, eloped with Hank Gibson, the neighbor boy. Robert met his death in a horse runaway. Dessie took pneumonia and won a hand-to-hand battle with death.

When I turned eighteen, you drove me in your coach to the homestead of Charles and Rebecca and I retrieved some rich heirlooms for Effie, determined to get them back to her by Christmas. And we made it!

We became confederates in easing Effie's heartaches, since you had lost a "bent-winged angel" from your own family and your tender feelings remained. Thank God, you understood!

Will we ever forget our return from the untamed Mexico land when we found Effie crying in the woodshed? (That's another memory I would like to blot out.) Life had become nearly intolerable for her in my absence. Remember the pretty quilts that were in the barrel we brought back? Effie had **prayed** for cover. I wept to think she had not slept warm a winter of her life.

In reading the key chapters of my life a second time, I'm finding some details I missed with the first reading.

Perhaps matters would have gone on in this tangled mat and Effie would have been cut away with Mother's scissors of judgment, relegating her to an institution for demented humanity, had not my baby sister Sally been born and involved in the fire. Sally was the favorite of the entire Harris brood. Being the tenth, Papa called her his "tithe baby."

God certainly sent you to me at life's crucible. The scene telescopes closer and clearer, bringing

24

into view that day six months ago when you last visited our home. Effie, exiting her woodshed habitat, saw the wind pick up a live coal from under the washpot and roll it beneath the wicker carriage where Sally was sleeping while Mother did the washing. Mother had stepped inside with an armload of dried clothes from the clothesline.

How did Effie ever manage it? With those uncooperative arms, she swept Sally from the buggy and fled to the house, scarcely escaping the flames herself. Mother, filled with bitter resentment, lunged at Effie, prying Sally from her unyielding grasp. That's when Effie fell and got that nasty scar on her face.

We were on our way there (by intuition, remember) when we saw the smoke and arrived in time to put out the fire that had spread to the woodshed and destroyed it.

Papa, seeing the smoke and flames, ran from the field in panic, supposing Sally to be trapped in the burning buggy. Dessie, on her way home from school, witnessed the whole panoramic scene.

We missed a great part of the grand finale when Mother learned what really happened. But as we stepped through the back door, sooty and disheveled, we saw something neither of us will ever forget. I can see Mother now holding Effie in her arms, kissing away her tears and suffering, doing her best to mend those years of rejection. That was the day my dream came true! Mother had at last accepted our "bent-winged angel."

I'm sure if Uncle Charles had lived—had re-

turned from California with his cache of gold—
the river of life would have followed a different
stream-bed. In place of the rocks and falls and ed-
dies would have been a gentle flow of comfort. I
seldom dwell on might-have-beens, but in place of
this delapidated brown shack would have been a
stately ranch house, with conveniences bespeaking
prosperity. And yet, could the end result have been
any richer? The last six months have been the best
of my life.

Now I stand at another crossroads. Although
I have been helping Papa with the spring planting,
my heart is not in farming. I'm sorry to say I have
caught myself actually loathing the stinginess of
the earth and sky here in Central Texas. I see no
future in this way of life for me. Papa merely ekes
out a meager existence.

Surely there's more to life than a gamble of
crops against the elements. The stakes are too high.
I've seen the disappointment in Papa's eyes and
the despair on Mother's face enough to know that
there's got to be a better way.

My present ambition is to build a grand room
onto this old house for Effie before I set out to seek
my fortune. Then my mission here will be complete.

Give the Brownings my regards without putting any notions in Charlotte's head about me!

I trust that you are in health and that I may
hear from you soon.

> As always, your faithful friend,
> Joseph Harris

Jim folded the pages and wiped a tear from his eye with a rough hand accustomed to the reins and whip. He knew that now was the opportune time to turn the coach driving over to Joseph. He had been right in his decision. He remembered what wise Solomon had said, "To everything there is a time and a season." Joseph was ready.

He laughed at the thought of how surprised Joseph would be at the news of the upcoming wedding.

Chapter 3

Heart Search

*E*ffie awoke to the pounding of hammers. Work had begun on her room.

"Effie!" Dessie shouted above the den. "You're to have th' biggest an' best room in th' whole house. Lucky, lucky you!"

"Yes, an' it'll be cool in th' summers an' warm in th' winters," Martha added, as if to explain away the strange lopsided effect the new south appendage gave the whole unsightly structure. "That's what matters most."

"Let's go outside an' watch, Effie." No grass grew under Dessie's feet. Effie followed with hasty, halting steps. The miracle of construction, like the fitting together of a giant jigsaw puzzle with its matching wooden pieces, thrilled her.

"H-how c-can I t-thank you e-enough?" Effie asked Joseph as she sat mesmerized in the shade of the giant, leafy oak and watched him put the split-log siding on her spacious room.

"After what you have done for this family, Effie—especially Mother—I couldn't build a room deserving of you even if I could line it with gold. But we'll both thank God that He answered our prayers."

"Y-yes!"

A week later, Joseph was down to the finishing touches. He found Martha sprinkling clothes, dipping her fingers into a bowl of water and flicking it onto the stiffly starched shirts, rolling them into a ball, then placing them in the clothes basket to dampen for ironing. "I want Effie to have a nice rug and a stove for heat," he told her. "Could you go into town with me to help choose the rug?"

Martha's dripping fingers stopped shaking, little balls of water forming on their tips. "I'm afeared to leave, Joseph," she said slowly. "Sarah's time is about due fer th' baby. Th' moon's changin' tonight, an' that sometimes affects a birthin'. I might be needed here any little minute."

"I want to please Effie with the color and all. . .a man's not too good at. . ."

"Why don't you take Effie along an' let 'er fetch 'er own as pleases 'er?"

"That's a good idea. After all, it's her room."

"But Joseph. . . ."

"What's your worry now, Mama?"

"It's my thinkin' you need to be savin' yore money again' th' day you'll be takin' a wife fer yerself."

Joseph brushed away her concern with a self-conscious chuckle. "I'm apt to be as old as Jim Collins before I take that step. I'm not thinking about marrying for a good long time. Why, who'd have me anyhow?"

"You never know what tricks yer heart might play, Joseph, an' you wouldn't want to be all spent out if'n you fall in love sudden-like. 'Tain't impossible."

A shadow crossed Joseph's sun-bronzed face. Martha had hit a sore spot, a chink in his armor. "Just how does a person tell, Mother, when he meets the right one to take to wife?"

"Well, seems to me you'd jest nat'ally *know*, Joseph."

"I've met a lot of nice girls, but none fetch my heart," Joseph confessed. "There's Sissy Rhodes in The Springs. She's a pretty girl with nice manners and good raising. I chide myself for not sparking her, but my heart isn't in it. How can you pursue something when your heart lags behind? Then there's Eunice Gibson down the road. You and Papa like her. She's close to home and lots of fun at parties. Not bad looking either. Her freckles and upturned nose would make her plumb cute to most boys. Maybe she's more like a sister. The romance part is missing. And then there's Charlotte Browning in the Territory—the one Jim has picked out for me. She has a charming personality and good qualities. She's an only child, but completely unspoiled. I hate to disappoint Jim, but Charlotte somehow isn't suited to me. I've met no one that I'd want to live with for the rest of my life."

"You sound mighty too-choosy."

"Seems to me it'd pay to be choosy about something as permanent as marriage. Marriage is forever. Life's a mighty long journey to travel a bumpy road."

"That's well said. But don't be frettin' yerself. Yore young yet, Joseph. . .only twenty-one."

"Closer to twenty-two, but no closer to knowing what

31

I want to do with my life," Joseph sighed, and turned to go.

"Time will bring answers, son. An' time will bring along th' right one yer way, too. Trust ole Father Time. Hain't never seen nuthin' he didn't solve. Can't rush 'im, though. Time's what you need."

"Maybe and maybe not. Anyhow, tell Effie to get ready for a trip to town tomorrow. Dessie can go along too since it's Saturday and she'll be out of school."

The two roosters, Elijah and Elisha, were heralding the approach of the crown of dawn when Joseph stirred. Time was in short supply. Jim would be putting in his appearance presently. Thinking about Jim brought vague unresolved thoughts into Joseph's mind that were like an unfinished project, a building incomplete in his soul.

Oh, yes, he remembered, it concerned love. But of course! I can ask Jim how love "happened." Is it sudden? Deliberate? Happenstance? What inner signal triggers this thing called romance? Jim, recently felled by Cupid's arrow, will have some answers. Joseph could hardly wait to talk to him!

Martha heard Joseph's slight movement and got up hastily to prepare breakfast and pack a lunch for him and the two girls.

"Th' day's jest knockin' itself out fer perfectness fer a trip," Martha greeted him when he passed through the kitchen to the wash basin to wash his face.

"I hope it stays that way. You know the old saying, 'If you don't like Texas weather, just wait five minutes,' " laughed Joseph. "Do you need anything from town, Mother?"

"Yes. Some darnin' needles. I'll be needin' to do some

sewin' when Sarah's baby gets here. An' get me some white thread, too. An' a little dab o' satin ribbin if'n Missus Webster has any."

"Does Papa need anything?"

"He needs to go afishin' an' get some relaxin'. Fetch 'im some fishin' hooks. I'll tell 'im I'm ahankerin' fer a mess o' fish. I don't like to see 'im all-workin' an' no-playin' like he's been doin' here lately."

Joseph readied the horses and wagon, then lifted Effie gently onto the springboard seat while Dessie swung her gangling legs up over the side in one nimble leap.

"Take careful care o' Effie," Martha warned.

"My life for hers, Mother," Joseph pledged, winking at Effie. "I'll have her back by the end of the day, rug, furnishings and all." The horses, Adam and Eve, started with Joseph's "giddy-up," and Effie waved an uncooperative hand to Martha, who was framed in the doorway wearing her frayed, checkered apron. Without her traditional apron, Effie supposed, Martha would feel immodest.

The thrill of the flawless morning infused Effie's entire being, plunging her into reverent silence. *What was it about a sunrise that made a person feel so close to the Creator?* she wondered.

No amount of breathtaking scenery could keep Dessie quiet for long, however. "I believe there ain't nuthin' prettier than th' fields o' bluebonnets in Texas in th' spring!" she exuded. "Don't you think so?"

Effie looked over the blue sea of flowers and agreed wholeheartedly, but Joseph's mind, not heeding the landscape, still groped for answers to Jim's sudden decision to marry. Only when Dessie called his name did he bring himself to concentrate on her chatter.

"Joseph, did you know that God is awful *extravagant*?"

"How so, Dessie?"

"Well, look how *many* flowers He planted! If it'd been me, I'd have planted maybe a few here and there in little rows. But God scattered flowers *everywhere*—all over the hills and fields and valleys. Just look!"

"You have a sermon fit for a parson there, Dessie."

"An' think about th' stars! He didn't just put one here an' there, but He splashed millions of them all across th' nighttime sky for us."

"And when He got ready to send us a special sister, He didn't send us just *anybody*, He sent us Effie!" Joseph grinned down at the contented girl at his side, grateful that the old hurts were mended.

"T-thank y-you," she murmured.

"Joseph, I don't really want you to go off on th' stage." Dessie was honest to a fault.

"Oh, but I'll be coming back often."

"Promise?"

"Cross my heart."

"But you might find a girl on the stagecoach an' get married like Jim did."

Joseph threw back his head and laughed gustily. "Coach drivers don't fall in love with passengers, you funny little goose!"

From store to store, the three shoppers trudged, selectively choosing furnishings for the new room. Joseph spared no expense, having saved his earnings for this moment. He had made a pact with himself ten years ago, and today that contract would be fulfilled. He was taking care of Charles's angel as he had promised to do.

In the city Mercantile he met Sissy Rhodes. Her wide white skirt swirled and rustled as she whirled about eagerly. "Joseph! It's a pleasure to see you again!" Her eyes lighted with gladness at the chance meeting. "And these are your sisters?"

"Yes. This is Dessie and Effie."

Her polite gesture of greeting took in both of the girls with not the slightest chagrin at Effie's affliction. "You have two beautiful sisters, Joseph," she said as she smiled her most gracious smile. The kindness impressed Effie, but Dessie's eyes rested with ravishment on Sissy's expensive clothes.

"She's rich!" she whispered to Effie.

"And s-sweet," added Effie.

There's one point in her favor, Joseph told himself as he evaluated the young lady. *She's not ashamed of Effie.*

"Father is giving me a graduation party out at Flat Top Ranch the last day of next month," she said demurely. "Jerry Redd will be bringing his guitar and Flynn Sides his violin, and we'll have a sing. We need your baritone. I'd be greatly honored to have you attend."

"The pleasure would be mine, I'm sure," Joseph bowed slightly, "but I'm afraid I'll be leaving before that date."

"You're. . .leaving?" Her disappointment was perceptible.

"Yes, I'm taking a job as a stagecoach driver, running from Central Texas to the Caprock stop in the New Mexico Territory."

"How. . .how interesting!" Sissy's composure rebounded slowly after suffering the setback. "Will the job be. . .permanent?"

35

"I'm not sure."

"I hope not. For personal reasons perhaps." Her eyes twinkled becomingly.

"The present driver, a good friend of mine, is getting married soon and we have yet to work out the details." This bit of information was given simply to fill the awkward silence.

"How nice. For your friend, I mean. At any rate, you'll be returning periodically?"

"To see these sisters, I'm sure," Joseph gestured toward Dessie and Effie who were politely examining a counter of trinkets nearby.

"I had hoped you'd find employment here in The Springs." Even as she spoke, Sissy sensed the futility of her words. Joseph was slipping from her grasp—Joseph, the good-looking, personable young man whom even her mother approved of. "But perhaps you'll drop us a line of correspondence now and then?"

"The future remains unpredictable, I'm afraid." Joseph knew he would not be writing to Sissy.

As they went their separate ways, Joseph wondered uneasily, *why did that informal meeting disturb me? And why was I so relieved when she took her leave?*

Like a veteran interior decorator, Effie selected a delicate rose-patterned rug, soft and elegant. Martha's suggestion to bring Effie was truly a masterpiece of wisdom. The purchase of the pot-bellied iron stove was left to Joseph, and a nightstand and accessories were chosen by Dessie. The shopping entourage recessed with bags of popcorn and glasses of cool lemonade. "C-can h-heaven be any b-better?" Effie asked comically.

While thus engaged in refreshments, Joseph espied

a horse galloping into town at a fast clip. The rider reined up at the adjacent doctor's office, his hair rumpled by the wind. "Why, that's Hank!" Joseph exclaimed, hurrying across the ruts of Main Street. "Something wrong, Hank?"

"Just Sarah. She needs th' doctor. Th' baby's on th' way!"

"Is everything. . .all right?"

"Accordin' to your mother, everything's normal. It's just scary, havin' your very first young 'un. Excitin', too!" Hank looked pale and shaken as he rushed into the building, intent on his mission and giving heed to little else. He left his horse ground-tied, its gaunt sides showing evidence of the hard run.

Jim getting married. . .Hank approaching fatherhood . . .Matthew in love with the gorgeous daughter of Pastor Stevens. . . Strange emotions struggled deep in Joseph's chest. *Is life ignoring me or vice versa? Should I run back and tell Sissy Rhodes that I will write her after all?*

The trio lunched at the lovely Steele Creek Campground amid the giant walnut trees and the crystal, flowing springs. There Martha's ham sandwiches and sugar cookies met their fate. The trees had stood for eons, sheltering weary pilgrims, and the rivulet had given to them her liquid music. But today, Joseph hardly noticed the intoxicating surroundings. His mind probed deeply into his soul. Perhaps the proverbial spring was turning his fancy lightly to disturbing thoughts of love.

Hours later, as he neared home, Joseph saw nineteen-year-old Eunice Gibson standing beside the road, waving her slat bonnet to them. Against the backdrop of wildflowers and picket fence, her slight frame looked

37

fragile and dainty. He called the horses to a stop.

"We're Uncle Joseph and Aunt Eunice!" she exploded, her freckled face aglow with a radiant, girlish grin and her hair askew. "Don't that sound great?"

"Have we a niece or nephew?" inquired Joseph with "uncle-ish" pride.

"A beautiful niece. She's the prettiest baby in the world and they named her Sally Rebecca Gibson! She's not nearly as heavy as Maw's ten pound sack o' sugar. Your mother said I was to go over an' help Dessie with supper an' see that Effie got plenty to eat." Joseph took her hand and helped her onto the wagon seat. It was a small, womanly hand just right for guiding a home.

Henry met the wagon to help Joseph unload. "Well, how does it feel to be grandpa?" greeted Joseph. The rapture on Henry's face gave him away.

"It's th' best feelin' in th' whole world, Joseph," Henry beamed. "I jest couldn't be none prouder! It's like bein' a papa double. This little 'un'll always be 'Little Sarah' to me. Th' ongoin' o' life is all a part o' God's big plan. Only when yore older, you can see it plainer. An' I shore like His idee. A *grand*baby is *grand* all right. They named it perfect."

Seeing Eunice in the clean, checkered apron presenting a warm and homey picture made Joseph the more uncomfortable. As a homemaker, she would be so "right." Her presence brought along sunshine and her sharp wit kept laughter alive throughout the evening. *She'd make somebody a good little wife. But could I ever think of her as anything other than a cousin, even though we are unrelated?*

He found himself drawn to her cheerfulness as she

38

rocked a sleepy Sally, in the setting room. "I'll help you with puttin' down th' rug an' arrangin' Effie's room when I get Sally to sleep," she offered, devoid of self-consciousness. "It's a wonderful room you built, Joseph!" The compliment made him feel warm inside.

Together they put up the low bed Joseph had made for Effie's convenience. Effie brought out her appliqued and embroidered coverlets, exquisitely pieced and quilted by relatives she had never known, saved for this moment. Dessie arranged the ironstone washbowl and pitcher on the sculptured marble-top washstand. Joseph positioned the friendly black heater in one corner on its three claw feet.

"Oh!" breathed Effie in exultation. As darkness settled over the whole, the glow of the lamp transformed the room into an enchanted queen's chamber, atmospheric and tranquil. Joseph's heart had known few moments of satisfaction superior to this. He hoped to provide such a chamber for his bride someday and almost grasped a feeling of romance. . .but again it eluded him. The magic something was just out of his reach.

He walked Eunice home in the twilight, his heart mellow and searching. *I'll leave the door open, and perhaps love will steal in,* he reasoned. The accomodating moon lent her encouragement in full to would-be lovers.

They stopped by Hank's and Sarah's for a peak at the new niece. "Won't it be fun watching her grow?" Eunice looked at Joseph, her sweet face full of motherly yearning.

"I. . .I guess I'll be gone most of the time."

"Where are you goin', Joseph?" She impulsively touched his arm. He had an urge to turn and flee.

"Jim Collins is getting married, and I'm taking his coach route in about a month."

Is it my imagination? he asked himself, suddenly startled. Or is Eunice crying?

Chapter 4

The New Job

The smell of freshly baked gingerbread permeated the whole house and wafted out to the front porch where Jim was welcomed by the Harris family.

"But you promised you'd wait an' marry me!" objected Dessie, still miffed at Jim's matrimonial intentions. None of Martha's dark looks inhibited Dessie's blunt outburst.

"Call the parson and we'll get married," teased Jim with mock sincerity. "I'll shuck all my other plans if you'll elope with me tonight. I need somebody to keep my house, and you're about as pretty as the one I've chosen. Can you cook?"

"I have to finish *grade* school first!" complained Dessie, mortifying her mother. "But you could'a waited!" She disappeared into the house, and one by one the other children went back to their play.

41

Joseph sat astraddle a cane-bottom chair backwards, facing Jim in the porch swing. "You're ready to take the route?" Jim asked, his voice masking a plea.

"Effie's room is finished, and I'm ready."

Jim's tension eased. "Good! I. . .things are going better than I had dared to hope."

"You were afraid I wouldn't take the coach?"

"I wasn't sure. And if you didn't, that would delay my plans. You might say I'm a bit selfish. But I've got to give it to you straight and as a friend, Joseph. You'll need to think of coach driving as a short-term vocation. The future is a dead-end trail. Probably a bigger gamble than farming."

"You mean you'll be climbing back on the box after your honeymoon?"

"No. The railroad is slicing across the country with amazing speed. They'll soon put the coaches out of business. Who would take a dusty, crowded, two-week coach ride when a train can cover the same distance in two *days*?"

"And the fares are competitive?"

"Very. The mainline stages are suffering. Some have already quit. The private lines like ours will make it another year or so possibly. We can say you'll be in the last stages of the last stage."

"Almost seems unfair, doesn't it?"

"We have to bow to progress, Joseph. We're colliding head-on with the twentieth century and we'll see many changes. Someone has even begun to talk about the possibility of a horseless carriage. Can you believe it? Some folks say it won't appeal to the public, but I say it will, sooner or later. And coaches will be an outdated thing

42

of the past. But you'll still consider taking the route, won't you?"

"Yes. A year of driving will probably cure me anyhow!" Joseph chuckled. "I hear it takes years to be a good driver, and since I don't have years, I can never hope to achieve the fame of my predecessor."

"I say either you're cut out for the work by nature or you're not. I take driving seriously and leave the shouting and whip-cracking to the showoffs. 'Nothing to prove, nothing to lose,' I always said."

"I guess it remains to be seen if I'm a born driver. But there are some basics?"

"A few simple, sensible rules that any levelheaded person can learn. We'll start on that tomorrow."

After supper, the younger children vied for Jim's attention. As usual, he showered them with gifts and candy. Joseph held his peace, waiting for Jim to bring up the subject of his bride, but Jim offered no information. Joseph studied him, weighing his words and actions. *He is the same old Jim in some ways. In other ways, hard to define, he has added an intangible dimension of. . .what is it? Placidness. . .maturity. . .contentment?*

"Daybust comes early these days, Joseph. Can you be ready?" Jim asked when Martha had coaxed the smaller children to bed against their will.

"I probably won't sleep a wink tonight anyway," Joseph returned. "So I won't have to worry about waking up."

"We had hoped you'd stay a few days with us," Henry invited.

"I'm afraid this old heart won't let me stay long," Jim laughed. "When Jim makes up his mind about something, he wants to get on with it."

"Well, congratulations."

"We'll slip out without bothering you," Jim told Henry and Martha, but both insisted on making the pre-dawn arousal to see them off. Joseph kissed Martha tenderly and gave Henry a bear hug. "I'll be checking back in a few weeks. Take care of my angel—and the new grandbaby!" Once in the coach, he didn't look back.

"It feels good to leave without worrying about Effie, doesn't it?" Jim mentioned as they took to the open road. The farming hamlet, candles and lamps aflicker, showed signs of a drowsy awakening as if reluctant to open its eyes.

"Mighty good."

"Things have been different since last fall, eh?"

"You said it! You know, I thought the first place Effie would want to visit when she obtained her reprieve would be the town's ice cream parlor or Sarah's and Hank's cottage. But was I surprised!"

"Let me guess. The school?"

"No. The church! She very nearly worships Pastor Stevens. Mother promised to let her get baptized when the river warms up. Afraid she'll get pneumonia. Effie asks every week if it's warm enough yet."

"Never heard of anyone getting sick from being baptized."

"I never have either, but Mother's overprotective. She wants to make sure Effie lives long enough to repay her for saving Sally's life."

They passed the school, the church, the parsonage. "Matthew's still in love with Pauline?"

"Yes, sir. He has it bad."

Now that the subject had drifted to courtship, Joseph anticipated a review of Jim's own romance, but was again disappointed. Jim was strangely mute. "Are you ready for our first lesson in coachmanship?" he asked abruptly, all business.

"I've so much to learn so fast, I guess I'd better get started."

"The first rule of thumb is to go over every strap and chain, feel the bridles and collars, and check the bits. A rough bit or twisted leather can cause big problems. Remember to grease the axles frequently to keep the wheels from getting too hot on the trail."

"Yes, sir."

"Your most important possession as a driver is your rawhide whip. It's worth a mint of gold to you. I have a very good one and I'll pass it on to you."

"Many thanks. It pays to have friends, I see."

"Remember that your horses' best gait is a trot; the worst is a gallop. And, in case of a runaway, pull the team into a wide circle, then tighten the circle until they come to a standstill."

"Wait! You're going too fast. Can I remember all this?"

"It'll come back to you when you need it."

"What about baggage limits?"

"Each passenger is allowed forty pounds of luggage. Charge four bits a pound for any extra they insist on taking. Meal stops should not exceed thirty minutes. A lot of time can be lost at stagestops. Business has slacked off considerably since the trains. I could count on making sixty dollars a month several months ago, but you won't collect that now. Some of the coach stops haven't

45

the most comfortable accommodations, but all have a place to sleep."

"You don't carry a gun?"

"I have a loaded gun in the front. I just don't advertise it. I keep it out of sight at all times."

"Couldn't you have made more money driving mainline? Did you ever consider it?"

"I had the chance, but I turned them down. I like being my own boss and having my own vehicle. The mainline coachhouses are rowdy, with a lot of drinking and gambling. I don't drink. Never have. I've seen a lot of good men fall to the habit."

"My own grandfather let drink destroy him."

After a silence suggested the end of the first lesson, Joseph cleared his throat. Now was as good a time to ask as any. "Is this. . .this marriage of yours a sudden impulse, Jim?"

Jim's mustache danced in amusement. "I guess you could call it that."

"Finally found someone you love better than the stage?"

"Yep. Finally. I'd about given up on myself."

"Must be *some* lady."

"You got that right."

"You'll be. . .married right away?"

"After this one last trip back to Santa Fe. I told her I'd give her one final chance to change her mind." Joseph waited for Jim's joking laugh, then sensed this statement was no joke. Jim was dead serious.

"And yourself?"

"My mind is made up. I've never been more positive about anything. And remember, you're to be my best man when it happens."

"In Santa Fe?"

"No. I plan to be married at the Caprock Stagestop. Mr. Browning holds license as a J.P. and the place is like a second home to me."

"And I would dare to say that you'll have Charlotte Browning participating in the wedding somewhere?"

"I'd planned on it. If you don't mind. How'd you guess?" A gleam of mischief played at the corners of Jim's eyes.

Joseph groaned, doubting that Jim's teasing had remained onesided. He hardly relished the encounter with Charlotte under these conditions. Then he asked offhandedly, "She's still single, then?"

"And just as charming as ever!" A millennium wouldn't change Jim.

Unanswered questions still badgered Joseph. *How long has Jim been acquainted with his future bride? What precipitated such an impromptu decision? His sister's death, perhaps? His passing youth? How can I ask these questions discreetly? Jim in love?* He pondered the idea at length. It seemed absolutely incredible.

"How does it feel to be in love, Jim?" Joseph had to know, regardless of how rude and prying his question might seem to his best friend.

Jim was silent for awhile, meditative. "I've always been poor at words of the heart, Joseph. And it's not easy to explain what has happened inside of me. I just feel like the luckiest man alive. And don't worry—this isn't infatuation. It's real. . .and sacred. I'm so *sure* of my feelings. I miss her every minute we're apart. Life is not complete —can never be complete—without her beside me. After

47

my sister died, I was all my family there was left and it was an empty, lonely feeling. It was then I *realized* that I was madly in love—that I'd been in love for a long time, in fact, and just didn't recognize the symptoms for what they were. I'm trying hard to keep my elation in check until I know that she's one hundred percent sure about me."

Joseph had Jim talking now and wasn't willing to let him stop. "Don't you think she is as much in love with you as you are with her?"

"Yes, I *think* so. But perhaps it's just because I want so badly to believe that. You see, I must be certain and there's one more hurdle. . .challenge. . .decision—I don't know what to call it—that I want to give her plenty of time to consider. Marriage is for always, you know."

"Will she. . .can she. . .have that decision made when you get back?"

"Shortly thereafter, anyway."

Joseph failed to unravel the mystery. But, of course, he had never been in love. "Jim, if this lady of yours changes her mind, she's crazy."

"If she changes her mind, *I'll* go crazy," Jim laughed.

"And you'll keep on driving?"

"Yes. Right off into the ocean!"

Joseph cut his eyes toward Jim. Jim was smitten! "She won't change her mind, Jim."

"Thanks, buddy. I've never heard sweeter words in my life. Keep me fed on that ambrosia."

"I'll see that she doesn't change her mind," threatened Joseph. "Because I want your driving job!"

"You're welcome to it."

"I don't believe you're even grieving about parting

48

with the road."

"I'm not. Are you ready for your second lesson?"

"Ready!"

"Then trade places with me and take the reins. It's time for you to drive awhile. And Joseph. . ."

"Yes, sir?"

"I have a bit of sage advice for you that you won't find in the books."

"What's that, Jim?"

"You're young and handsome, and some of the female passengers will use cunning to trap you. Not all women who ride coaches are. . .virtuous. You'll have to be mighty careful."

"I'll not give them a chance at my heart, Jim."

"I wish I could believe that."

Was Jim speaking from experience? Was he trapped on the trail?

"The Brownings put a little caption on this trip for me." Jim's eyes twinkled.

"What's that?"

"The Last-Stage of Love."

Chapter 5

A Different Charlotte

"It looks as if Charlotte is expecting us," Joseph mused, as he gracefully brought the horses to a halt with a flourish and clatter of hooves at the Caprock stage stop. Charlotte stood in the doorway of her father's store, dressed in an attractive sprigged calico frock.

"I told her you'd be coming along with me," Jim grinned. "And by the way, that was quite an impressive stop you made. Fit for a king."

"Thanks. I'm loving driving better everyday. I'll soon be addicted."

A blushing Charlotte waved to them, creating the impression that she could scarcely hold herself back from running to the coach to extend her personal greetings. *Jim's right,* decided Joseph reflectively. *She's prettier than ever. I'll have to be on my guard. My heart isn't for sale or lease.*

Jim went inside, allowing Joseph to care for the team by himself; he needed the experience. He would be close by in case Joseph summoned him. Joseph felt only blessed relief to be out of Charlotte's range of vision, however temporary the respite.

"Supper's coming right up," Mrs. Browning beamed her welcome when Joseph entered the house. "My! It's good to have you two home!" Jim had disappeared to his room to freshen up for the evening meal.

Mr. Browning greeted Joseph with a hearty handshake. "I believe your three-year absence has only made you handsomer," he complimented. "You've made quite a man of yourself." Charlotte smiled pleasantly, keeping her place with ladylike dignity.

She's trying a new tactic, Joseph told himself. *Subtle. But I'll be wary.*

Throughout the evening meal, Charlotte showed quiet reserve and proved much more mature than on Joseph's last visit. As a result, he began to relax, letting down his guard. She politely included him in the table conversation, asking solicitiously about Effie and the rest of his family.

"They're all well, and I'm a new uncle," he told her. "Sarah has a baby girl."

"Congratulations!" she offered modestly, refraining from sending overt attention in his direction. A strangely different Charlotte with her subdued manner allayed Joseph's dread of spending the night there or acknowledging to himself that Caprock would be a regular stop in his new work. His lion of apprehension became a lamb. If Jim could just be trusted not to play matchmaker, Joseph supposed he could be comfortable.

"We hear you'll be taking Jim's route, Joseph, and we'll be seeing much more of you," Mrs. Browning mentioned. "There's certainly no one we'd rather see take Jim's place."

"I'm afraid no one could ever take Jim's place," Joseph replied humbly. "I'm stepping into big boots. But I'll try to make a paltry substitute."

"He'll do honorably," protested Jim. "Charlotte, you saw that superb stop he made a while ago when we came in. I couldn't have done better myself, now could I?"

Charlotte blushed again, turning her soft eyes quickly from Jim to Joseph, but only smiled and murmured, "It was a nice stop."

Presently Mr. Browning steered the conversation to the rapid development of the area. "With the railroad coming, we'll be booming," he said. "Can you imagine Caprock *populated?*"

"And has the land that Uncle Charles staked claim on been sold?" Joseph queried.

"No, not yet. It has a good water supply and plenty of timber, though, and I suspect someone will discover its worth before long."

"The land has always intrigued me," Joseph admitted, remembering too late that he must give Charlotte no reason to set her heart on him. "It seems a part of me, somehow. I am thinking of buying it myself."

"Nothing would please us better! You could probably get it cheap right now. Might be that you could even work something out with the Federal Land Men to take up where Charles left off on the claim. He only lacked six months in getting his papers. I think, in fact, they have lowered the time required for living on the land."

"Do you feel that it could be turned into a profitable ranch?"

"Yes, I do, Joseph. Plenty of mustang horses running wild, free for the taming. They make good stock. Tough animals, durable. They can be trained to do most anything. Once you win their trust, you have it forever. If I was a young man, I'd jump at the chance." Charlotte listened with growing interest, but said nothing.

"But wouldn't you need to get, ah, a wife in that case, Joseph?" Jim's mustache twitched. "You know. . ."

"I'll have to drive awhile to get enough money to support myself, much less anyone else," stammered Joseph, trying to head off Jim's too-obvious implication. "I spent all I had saved on Effie's room."

"But you should go ahead and check into the land. . .before someone else beats you to the draw," Mr. Browning pressed. "I'd hate to see you lose it. It. . .after all Charles went through. . .I'd like to see it stay in the family. And I think Charles would too."

"I'll check into it, Mr. Browning."

"Will. . .will you be coming to the big wedding, Joseph," Charlotte asked coyly.

"Jim seems to think he can't stand up without me," laughed Joseph.

"Oh, I'm sure he couldn't." The words leaped out eagerly and two bright pink spots painted Charlotte's cheeks. "Dad's going to perform the ceremony, you know."

"Jim told me."

"I think Charlotte is more excited about the wedding than Jim is!" Mrs. Browning teased.

"Well, it's not every day we have a famous wedding

at Caprock, Mother," Charlotte returned playfully, "with Joseph for a guest!"

"And this one's really special," Mr. Browning added. "It's my first since I got my license as Justice of the Peace."

"Daddy may get nervous and forget his lines," Charlotte said. "You may have to help him, Jim. You'll want to make sure he gets the 'obey' in there."

"Well, everything actually depends on the final decision of my lady," Jim said, looking not at all worried.

"Yes, I told him if his ladylove changed her mind, she's crazy," Joseph explained.

"And do you know what I said?" Jim winked mischievously at Charlotte. "I said if she changed her mind, I'd go crazy."

"Furthermore I asked him if he'd keep driving if she turned him down, and he said he would. . .right off into the ocean," Joseph continued, laughing.

"You'd think he was in love if you didn't know better." Now it was Charlotte's turn to banter with Jim. She cast a sideways glance at Joseph. "Love is a wonderful thing. Don't you think Jim seems happy, Joseph?"

"Very," Joseph replied. "And all I've got to say is that he deserves the best."

"We think he's getting the best," Mrs. Browning said proudly. It relieved Joseph's misgivings to know that a reputable family like the Brownings approved of Jim's choice of a bride. Undoubtedly, Jim had brought her here and introduced her to them. He could hardly wait to meet her himself—this lady with enough magic to turn a roadrunner to a homing pigeon!

"I feel like I know your whole family, Joseph."

Charlotte talked more freely now. The subject of Jim's wedding seemed to break the ice. "Jim tells me you have a brother who's in love, too." She lifted her eyes shyly.

Joseph squirmed. "Matthew's in love all right, but it'll be awhile before he can take a wife. He plans to go to college come fall."

Joseph wished to take no further chances with the topic of romance. Jim might make another unpredictable blunder. So as soon as he could unobtrusively do so, he excused himself to his room, not bothering to light the lamp. A feeling of sweet escape washed over him.

He left Jim to the pleasure of Mr. and Mrs. Browning and Charlotte. No other guests registered at the inn that night. He opened his window to the exhilarating atmosphere of the high plains and took a deep breath. The drone of voices and laughter drifted up from below. Doubtless they were planning Jim's wedding, where he would again be drawn unwillingly into Charlotte Browning's company, much to Jim's delight. He prided himself that he'd come through this night reasonably unscathed; his last conscious thought before drifting off to sleep was thankfulness that the Brownings knew and liked the woman his best friend planned to wed. . .when she made the "decision."

He had not slept so good in many a night. Jim had to knock on his door to awaken him. Newborn daylight yawned through the open window, and Joseph hastened into his clothes and boots to hitch up the horses for the trip to Santa Fe. Jim was anxious to be on the way.

Natural and unflustered, Charlotte came to share breakfast with them and see them on their journey. The soft blue robe she wore enhanced the blue of her eyes and made her strikingly beautiful. Joseph knew he could never explain to Jim why he held his heart back from such a lovely young lady as this. In fact, he did not know if he could expound the reasons to himself. To Joseph, life was a puzzle. Jim had attempted to explain it to him once, comparing it to a jigsaw puzzle's many-shaped pieces. "We pick a piece up and put it to one side when we can't find its rightful place," Jim said. "Sometimes we are tempted to discard it because it doesn't fit, but that would be foolish because it'll fit in the puzzle later on." Joseph wondered if Charlotte would ever fit into his life.

Just before Jim climbed onto the driver's box beside Joseph, Charlotte moved quickly to his side and whispered something in his ear. Jim smiled and nodded. As she raised her eyes to Joseph, her tender look grappled his heart. He hastened to lift the reins in an attempt to take flight. Charlotte waved her graceful, slender hand and blew a goodbye kiss toward the receding coach. *What am I running from?* Joseph rebuked himself. *My heart?*

Jim chuckled. "Those Brownings are just special. Like my own family."

"You were right about Charlotte, Jim. She's made a charming young lady. Changed a lot in three years. For the better."

"I knew you'd see it eventually!"

"Now, wait a minute. What did I say?"

"You simply stated an undeniable fact."

"Which doesn't mean that I have any future intentions. . ."

"Tell me, Joseph," Jim's face grew serious. "Don't you think you will ever want to marry Charlotte. . .in the future?"

57

"I am going to be completely honest with you, Jim. You're my best friend. I don't want to offend you by spurning your well-meaning attempts at matchmaking all these years. I appreciate your concern. But I can never marry Charlotte Browning. I'm not faulting her in the least. She's lovely, and I can't explain why, but somehow she's not suited to me as a *person*. I wonder, Jim, if there's something wrong with me. I seem to build a formidable fortress in my mind against even the loveliest of young ladies. Will I ever feel. . .love? I've never felt. . .a romantic attraction for anyone."

Jim laid a kindly hand on Joseph's muscled arm. "I understand, Joseph. I've been down your road. I promise not to pester you about Charlotte Browning anymore. What I've said already isn't fair. Forgive me. I know what real love is now, and someday, somewhere you will experience it for yourself. It'll probably come when you least expect it. . .as it did for me."

Chapter 6

Lilly

"*M*eester Jim. . .wife get soon. . .home he move. . .I keep ready." Lilly mumbled aloud to herself, a habit picked up since the death of her mistress left her with no one to talk to.

Lilly, half Indian and dark-skinned, came to attend his sister's family so long ago that Jim would never think of managing the household without her. She still struggled with language barriers, but her passion for housekeeping was relentless. Now she scrubbed the walls of the massive adobe house, starched every curtain, and polished the tile floors until her olive face reflected in them.

"Baby die. . .missus go too. . .Meester Jim now house man. . .good man he. . .take good wife," she talked on as she lifted the lid from the pot of bubbling soup on the cookstove, which smelled of wild marjoram. "Might home come today. . .Meester Jim. . .I be glad. . .Any day. . . ."

At that moment, the coach swung in from the east. "There's my place, Joseph." Jim waved a hand in an arch toward the sprawling, flat-roofed adobe building, sunbleached white. It squatted solidly on the ground, surrounded by a green carpet of grass. Joseph caught his breath. A cloud hung over the top of the setting western sun, resembling a round-faced man wearing a hat, taking his leave to leap over the majestic Sangre de Cristo mountains.

"Whew!" gasped Joseph. "I wish I had Sarah's artistic ability. I'd paint a picture. And what a picture it would be! I've never seen a sight lovelier!"

"In winter, the mountains are snow-capped. As you can see, my place sits in the lap of a mountain. Sis loved it. She named the place Cristo Haven."

"And I love it, too!"

"There's Lilly!" Jim waved cheerily to the flat-faced woman with a single blue-black braid of hair falling across one shoulder. "Dear, faithful Lilly! I can't imagine Cristo Haven without her."

Lilly joyously met them at the gate with childlike abandon, crushing Jim with a glad hug. *So this is the one,* Joseph thought, his heart plunging into a black abyss of depression. *She's at least twenty years older than Jim!* Her dark, laughing eyes showed utmost delight at Jim's homecoming. *But she loves him.*

Jim led the way into the house with Joseph tailing miserably behind. Inside, another surprise awaited Joseph. The spacious front room abounded with elaborate furnishings such as Joseph had never seen. Beyond the hall tree where he left his battered hat, a velvet love seat, carved with lion-head features, caught his eye. Shelves of books lined a short wall. *Wouldn't Effie love this?* A sweet potato plant, sprouting from a pottery jug in the window, sent long, leafy shoots around the facing to form a green trellis.

Fortunately, adaptability was one of Joseph's most admirable traits. It kept him from complete vertigo as his mind churned dizzily. He felt as though he had entered a new world with the dust of the old still clinging to his soul.

Jim's nose led him into the aromatic kitchen where he peeked into the pot of soup. "Yum! Smells heavenly, Lilly!" Jim was home now and totally relaxed. "You made this soup with me in mind, you old dear!"

"Meester Jim. . .marry. . .you know?" Lilly turned to Joseph with a grin that showed missing teeth. "Good man . . .Meester Jim."

"Yes," Joseph answered and wanted to add, *I'm happy for him,* but the words froze in his throat and refused to thaw out.

"I. . .house. . .keep good," she said simply. "Always . . .I Meester Jim like."

"Now be a good girl and dish us up some of your famous stew." Jim reached into the elegant china cabinet for bowls. "We're nigh starved." He patted Lilly's round brown arm.

Joseph followed about in a daze, not knowing what to do or say. If Jim noticed Joseph's confusion, he gave no indication of it. His mind was elsewhere. He whistled happily about the kitchen, getting in Lilly's way. "Lilly's a great cook, Joseph," he bragged, and one taste of the soup convinced Joseph that Jim was not exaggerating.

Jim turned to Lilly. "We'll be going back to Caprock

for the wedding the day after tomorrow, Lilly," he told her. "Tomorrow I'll take care of the business here so that everything will be in order when we return."

"Help. . .I can?"

"You can help by keeping our stomachs full, Lilly. I want Joseph to set his taster on some of your delicious bucket bread."

"A very good meal," Joseph complimented when he finished his soup. He saw that the praise pleased Lilly.

After supper, Jim picked up the gourd-shaped mandolin standing in the corner of the living room and began an off-chord rendition of "Yankee Doodle." Joseph had never seen him in higher spirits and hoped his own flagging mood was not discernable. He would be glad when the whole ordeal was over and he took to the driver's box of the stagecoach. *Let Jim handle his own problems! Let him marry whom he will!*

"We'll have the lettering changed on the coach tomorrow, Joseph," Jim paused and propped the instrument under his chin. "From Collins Transport Company to Collins and Harris Transport Company. How does that sound, driver?"

It was the first time Joseph had smiled since entering this second world. "Good!"

"My lady hasn't changed her mind, so when we get back to Caprock, the driving will be yours. For as long as you want it."

Joseph thought to sleep off his bitter unrest, but his mind spun long into the night. The feather mattress, down pillow, and satin comforter brought no solace. *You can't help but like Lilly. But Jim marrying an Indian woman who speaks only broken English? How could the Brown-*

ings approve so heartily? Of course white men sometimes took Indian wives, but this one was old enough to be Jim's mother! There on the frontier, such behavior was acceptable, but in the higher echelons of society, pure blood ancestry was much esteemed. Jim would be ostracized by people not a whit better than himself because of his choice of a wife. Even the government frowned on these unions.

Joseph had supposed that Jim would want children to propagate his name, and this woman was was well past the child-bearing age. *Which was fortunate!* The children born to such a wedlock would be dubbed "breeds" or "bloods" throughout their life, being accepted by neither their white nor red kinsmen. Joseph turned restlessly. *Something just isn't right. These two in love?*

When he awoke after a troubled dream that escaped his memory, the peace that had taken wings yesterday had not flown back. He supposed it had gone forever. The pangs of despair for Jim persisted. *Will I always feel it when I visit Jim in future years? Or will it disappear with time. . .and with good Indian cooking?*

Joseph heard the sound of Jim's rawhide boot soles on the tile floor and jumped up, feeling as though he hadn't slept a wink. Lilly had brewed a pot of fresh coffee, the best he had ever tasted. A vase of freshly cut flowers sat at the center of the table, and Jim was a rainbow of cheer. Lilly bustled about serving breakfast, all a-bubble. *If Jim is happy, why can't I accept it? It's his life, not mine. Tomorrow. . .*Joseph wanted to reach out and stay the hypnotic pendulum that rocked from side to side in the mantle's banjo clock. *Tomorrow we will return to Caprock for this mismatched marriage.*

"You. . .more egg. . .like?" Lilly asked Joseph, anxious to please.

"No, thank you."

Will this plump Indian woman dress in Indian attire for the wedding? What would she look attractive—or younger—in?

"I'll take you on a tour of our town while I'm catching up on my business," Jim was saying. "Lot of Indian history."

The tightness in Joseph's chest relented slightly when they were out of Lilly's presence. Unsuccessfully Joseph tried to drive the worry from his mind.

"What brought your family here?" he asked Jim. Courtesy demanded that he make conversation.

"The Santa Fe Trail. There used to be a monthly stage running along the north route between here and Independence, Missouri. My father drove the route before he got his own coach. He liked this place so well that he brought his family here. Ten years ago, the railroad reached the Lamy station, sixteen miles out. As of this year, the Santa Fe Railroad has nine thousand miles of track with connections to Chicago and Los Angeles. It's the world's longest railway system."

"Which meant the death of the Santa Fe Trail?"

"Exactly. Our city is now a shipping point for Indian wares, minerals, and farm products."

"This town's been here a long time, hasn't it?"

"Founded in 1609 by the Spanish. It was the center of Spanish-Indian trade for two hundred years. This little burg has always been a seat of government. The Palace of Governors was built in 1610 and has been occupied by Spaniards, Indians, Mexicans, and Americans in turn. See that old church?" He pointed toward a stately old vine-covered structure. "That's the San Miguel Mission, built in 1636."

"I'd love to show Effie those mountains."

"You must bring her out here to see me and. . ." Joseph waited, but Jim didn't finish. "Our altitude is seven thousand feet above sea level."

"What will you do for a living here?"

"I have plenty of land and can make good at farming. Anything'll grow in this climate. Beats anything you ever saw for cultivation. Wish we could sneak a little of it back to Central Texas."

Now Joseph felt real sympathy for Jim. *A vegetable farmer with an Indian wife. For a man like Jim, accustomed to the zest of the driving box, it would be tragic. Jim . . .a real gentleman. . . .*

"Excuse me while I drop in this little shop and pick up a piece of turquoise jewelry for Lilly." Jim dismounted. "She has worked hard for me. And you know how Indians love trinkets. She's Navajo."

Joseph grieved away the remaining hours in Santa Fe, missing the beauty of the golden sunsets. He welcomed departure day's light of morning. *Will Jim and Lilly ride inside the coach while I drive? Or will Lilly ride up on the high seat with Jim and me?* As a third party, he was certain to feel awkward.

But when leaving time came, Lilly made no effort to join the two eastbound men. She stood at the gate waving a large bronze hand.

"She's. . .not coming with you?" Joseph asked, puzzled.

"Lilly's not a traveling person. She's content to stay

right at home and see that everything is kept in order for me. Lilly's one in a million."

Now Joseph was indeed baffled. *How can Jim marry someone who is not there? Is there such a thing as marrying by proxy—like absentee voting?*

"But. . .but your marriage?"

"As soon as we get there! And boy, I can hardly wait!"

"You. . .er. . .have I ever met your. . .bride?"

"You've met her, Joseph. You've stayed under the same roof with her. But I didn't tell you who she was because I had to make sure about both of you. You know . . .sometimes absence makes the heart grow fonder. . . ."

"*Both* of *us*?"

"My principles would never allow me to undermine a friend, no matter how much I loved the lady. You said you'd never marry the lovely Charlotte Browning, so I'll go ahead with my plans to marry her myself!"

"Jim! You. . .you rascal!" Joseph brushed back tears of joyful relief that oozed from his unbelieving eyes. "*You* are marrying *Charlotte Browing*?"

"There's not really that much. . .age difference."

"That didn't enter my mind. I just. . .well, I just never *suspected* it, that's all."

"I knew you didn't. Do you remember as we left the Brownings' Tuesday morning, Charlotte ran out and whispered something in my ear?"

"I remember."

"And blew me a kiss?"

Joseph laughed teasingly, "Why, I thought that kiss was for me!"

"Make no mistake. It was *mine*!"

"Thank goodness!"

"But I had to wait until you came west to make sure Charlotte didn't still carry a torch for you after your three years' absence. She assured me she hadn't changed her mind. . .that it was still me she loved and wanted to marry. You did me a great favor when you told her I'd drive right off into the ocean if she jilted me!"

"I should have seen it! Why, her heart was in her eyes for you, Jim. I'm as blind as a bat when it comes to romance. I just never thought. . . ."

"That's what you get for not thinking, old pal. But you're happy for me?"

"Happy?! Why, Jim, I'm beside myself! Charlotte will make the most adorable friend-in-law in the world! I thought you were going to marry Lilly!"

"Lilly? *Lilly!* My *housekeeper?* I just hope you have enough *intelligence* to drive this coach!" Jim guffawed. "Whatever in the world made you think that?"

Joseph shrugged. "I'm good at jumping at conclusions."

"And missing the facts by a million miles."

"You and Charlotte are perfect for each other, Jim. And the Brownings are so pleased. . . ."

"While I was trying to convince you, I convinced myself."

"No wonder my heart was closed to Charlotte. She was meant for you all the time."

"I believe you've slowed down, Joseph. Either speed it up or let me drive!"

"*Charlotte Browning*. . .Jim, this is just too good to be true!"

Chapter 7

The Mortgage

"*My* garden's burnin' up, Henry. An' th' peaches er dryin' up in th' blooms. I won't be able to do no cannin' fer winter."

"Yes, Martha. If'n we don't get some rain in th' next few days, I'm afraid we're in trouble. Serious trouble."

"Crops ain't comin' up neither, er they?"

"No. They're witherin' up in th' fields."

"What we gonna. . . ?"

"Papa!" William looked flushed and disturbed. "Th' grass is all turnin' yellow. Where can I stake out Bossy to graze?"

"Take 'er down near th' river, Will. Tie 'er to a tree."

"An' whiles yore down there, William," Martha interjected, "would ye look fer some lamb's-quarter an' poke greens fer supper tonight?" Fewer and fewer varieties of food appeared on the Harris table of late, but the children never complained of the monotonous mush and milk menu.

Matthew stamped in at the back door, water bucket in hand. "Papa," he said worriedly, "look at this bucket! I tried to draw up some water and came up with mud on the bottom of it!"

"Th' well's goin' dry." Henry shook his head. "Thank God our property's close by th' river. We'll have to haul water fer ourselves an' th' animals, too. Won't be no easy job. But then we was never promised no bed o' roses in this life."

"I'd best bile th' drinkin' water, Henry. We don't want to chance no chills 'n fever from exposed water."

"Th' water's gettin' mossy 'round th' edges. Runnin' water's generally safe, but do as you like, if'n it'll make you feel safer."

"No chance o' th' river quittin' runnin' is there?" Martha asked anxiously.

"No, there'll always be some water in th' Brazos River. Never heared o' it runnin' plumb out. It's gettin' mighty low, though."

"You an' th' boys need to keep a check on them trotlines, Henry. A bait o' fish would shore help fill up empty plates."

In the days of stifling heat that followed, Martha dipped into her emergency stock in the cellar. Jars of scarce canned food, dried fruits, and pickled vegetables disappeared with frightening alacrity.

"With ten o' us eatin', our grub ain't gonna last long," she fretted to Henry. "Th' cellar's 'bout empty."

Effie heard Henry and Martha's low talks long into the night. Whatever their conversation involved, it was

70

painful, and although she did not understand the problem, she felt that the worries concerned her, too, for this was her family. She prayed that she might ease their tensions and made a special effort to be cheerful.

By the first of July, Henry knew that the cash crops were doomed. The supply of food from the previous year's stock was gone. Fish, eggs, milk, and mush sustained them.

"What'll we do, Henry?" Martha asked, tears threatening. "I dare not kill any more hens fer food till a few more grow a bit."

"We don't have much choice, Martha. Th' ground is crackin' open fer lack o' moisture. Pecans ain't fillin' out. Even th' *weeds* er wiltin'! We either mortgage th' place at th' bank fer money fer food an' supplies, er sit here an' starve to death!"

"I don't want us to mortgage th' place, Henry."

"Have you a better suggestion, Martha?"

"What's ever'body else doin'?"

"Th' same thing."

"Maybe we could jest sell off a few acres o' our bottom land an' keep th' rest title-clear."

"Nobody'd buy now with th' land beggin' a drink. Money's tight as a wedge all over th' state. I jest hope we can even get a mortgage on th' place."

"Couldn't we maybe borrow some money from Joseph to get us by?"

"Joseph spent all he had on th' new room fer Effie."

"That's what I feared. I tried to warn 'im."

"He wouldn't have it no other way."

"What about Matthew?"

"What little money Matthew's got saved up fer his

71

education wouldn't last us no time. We'd have to mortgage when it was all used up, anyhow. Six o' one, half dozen th' other.''

"A mortgage means if'n we don't get th' money to pay back in a certain time, we lose our home. . .th' new room Joseph built an' all?''

"That's what it amounts to, I'm afeared, Martha. But we'll have to take that chance. We ain't got no choice. We'll have to trust God to help us get it paid back. I'm th' man o' th' house an' I'm responsible not to let these children die o' hunger. We didn't make no garden, no fruit, an' ain't makin' no crops. Ain't never seen a year so thirsty.''

As feed grew scanty, the chickens laid fewer eggs. Bossy gave less milk, and what she did give was often weedy. Henry staved off the inevitable as long as possible.

Finally, he acquiesced. "Martha, we'll just have to do what we have to. If'n we lose our place, we gotta save our lives regardless. Get ready an' let's go to th' bank, an' pray we can get a loan. You'll have to sign th' papers with me. Yore name's on th' deed to this place same as mine.''

Martha donned her black crepe church dress, patched over in places, and best hat and went along with Henry. The bank in The Springs turned them down. "We're loaned out to our limit," the president apologized. They hastened on to Meridian.

The banker at the Bosque County Bank frowned. "You're the sixth man I've had asking for money this week," he said grudgingly. "Can't loan you much. Property isn't worth a plugged nickel right now, whether it has a house on it or not. If you defaulted, we'd lose. I can only loan for one year. If at the end of the year your crops are prospering and you need a three-month extension to harvest, we may be able to arrange for you to pay the interest and have the added time. Central Texas is hard hit, you understand."

Henry and Martha signed the mortgage for six hundred dollars. Martha's hand shook when she penned in her signature, as if she was signing her own death warrant.

"Now Martha, I know it ain't exactly normal, but I tell you what I'm gonna do," Henry explained when they left the bank. "I'm gonna give God a tenth o' this here borrowed money. Parson Stevens has got to live too. He put away our Robert an' he comes to pray fer us when we're sick, besides th' baptizin's. God'll come nearer stretchin' this money to meet our needs an' helpin' us to get it paid back to th' bank if'n we put Him first."

"As you say, Henry." Martha's hand still shook from holding the pen that seemed filled with ink of evil intent.

"An' get out th' list you brought. We'll stop in Th' Springs an' pick up enough supplies to last a few weeks anyhow."

"Yessir."

The list included a hundred pounds of dried beans, a hundred pounds of flour, two hundred pounds of potatoes, onions, cinnamon, vinegar and honey (for cough syrup), saleratus (baking soda), a barrel of molasses, twenty pounds of salt, oatmeal, coffee beans, one hundred pounds of sugar, peppercorns, sage, tea, sulphur, cocoa, fifty pounds of rice, matches, ink, sewing thread, coal oil for the lamps, mash for the hens, cow feed, and oats for the horses. Forty dollars of their precious mortgage money stayed in the merchant's coffers. "That leaves us five hundred dollars for th' year," Henry said. "Barring any unforseen expenses, we should make it fine." "We'll have to make a double crop next year to pay th' bank back an' live, too." reminded Martha. "What if'n we don't get no rain next year?"

"We'll have to pray fer rain," admonished Henry. "That's th' good Lord's business."

"An' if'n we don't get it, we lose our property?"

"I'm afeared so, but let's try not to think 'bout it now. It behooves us to be thankful we even got th' loan."

"We ain't never been in no predicament like this."

"No, we never had to borrow money afore."

"Seems most nigh sinful, spendin' money what ain't our'n by th' earnin'."

"We're doin' th' best we know, Martha. Now stop worryin'."

The unrelenting heat beat down oppressively on Martha's hat, and her black dress absorbed the sunshine, adding to her misery. They passed field after field covered with brown patches of blistered plant life. Henry motioned toward them. "See there. Th' whole countryside's sufferin'."

"It's a bad year all th' way 'round. Turrible year fer Miss Vivian to take out o' teachin'. If'n she coulda jest seen us through this drought."

"Yep. It's gonna be mighty hard to find another teacher to come in here under these conditions. It's shore been concernin' me. It's awful important fer young 'uns to have an education these days so's they don't have to go through life strugglin' like us with no book learnin'."

"Couldn't Brother Stevens fill in as teacher till we

74

could get somebody? He's bound to be mighty educated, th' way he reads those big Bible words."

" 'Twouldn't be right, Martha. That ain't his callin' an' th' kids that listened to him teach all week at school would lose respect fer listenin' to him preach on Lord's Day. God called him to preach, not teach school. I'd be agin' it even if'n everybody else was fer it."

"I see that wouldn't work, Henry. Yore right. A preacher hadn't ort to lower hisself to bein' a school teacher. My mind was jest reachin' fer straws. I so bad wanted Effie to get to go to school come fall."

"Our main problem is that th' government don't pay much in these here small schools. Unless'n a teacher has a supplement o' some kind like Miss Vivian an' her bank account, they're out o' luck to survive on th' pay they git. An', too, we don't have no housin' fer an outside teacher. Miss Vivian is one o' us an' had her own lodgin'. Whoever comes'll have to stay with someone, prob'ly the parson."

"Do you s'pose there might be someone lookin' fer work along th' stagecoach line? Might'n we post Joseph a letter to be on th' lookout fer us a teacher?"

"We wouldn't have nuthin' to lose by postin' Joseph a letter. He's bound to meet up with lots o' people goin' from place to place. An' he wouldn't send us no undesirable."

"I'll get Dessie to write him tomorrow."

"An' don't mention to 'im that we borrowed money on th' place. It'd jest plague 'is mind."

The mortgaged home came into sight. "Our'n an' th' bank's," Martha sighed resolutely. "An' it remains to be seen who wins out."

" 'Tain't a place nobody would bother to envy, but

75

it's home." Henry cast an anxious glance toward Martha. "Martha, soon's I get this wagon unloaded o' yore stuff, I'm goin' up to th' parsonage an' take Brother Stevens his sixty dollars."

"What's th' rush, Henry? You can take it to 'im Sunday."

"If'n I wait, th' devil'll talk me out o' it."

Chapter 8

Preparations For A Journey

"*N*ina, do you know where Grandma kept the key to her humpback trunk?" Amy asked the housekeeper of the eighteen-room mansion. "I want to see if I can find a picture of Aunt Annie."

"Why yes, Miss Amy. It's in the jewelry box on the vanity. Missus Margaret always put it there for safe keeping."

"Jonathan and I have decided we'd like to sell this place, Nina. Mr. Stafford has been leasing the land this past year, you know, and now he wants to buy it. We have the Browning homestead left to us by our own parents. It's small, but it's all we need. This estate is quite too large for the two of us to care for."

Amy sat down on the edge of the high four-poster bed. Out the chintz-curtained window, past the well-manicured lawn, her eyes rested on the gentle rolling hills beyond.

The carefully kept estate looked much as it did in Amy's earliest memory. The tall white columns supporting the upper balcony gleamed with fresh paint. She remembered as a child looking up and up at their dizzying heights, dwarfed by their altitude. Time had only enhanced the house's value and beauty. Selling it would be like bartering away a part of her childhood, but common sense dictated that it would be foolish to keep it for sentiment alone.

"There's only one problem. We must find Aunt Annie. She and her children are the only other living heirs."

"Finding Ann may be like finding a needle in a haystack, honey."

"But you know Jonathan, Nina. If it's there, he'll tear down the whole haystack to find it!" laughed Amy. "Since he has reached the age of majority, he feels it is his responsibility to find Aunt Annie and see if she is agreeable to selling her parents' home. I suppose you have no idea of her last known address?"

"No, I don't, Miss Amy. She went out west somewhere with her husband. So many others were going for the California gold back then. It was like an obsession—a mania. They just got caught up with the idea and couldn't get it out of their heads. More than a few were never heard of again."

"Mother said Grandma threw a royal fit when Aunt Annie left."

"Yes'm, she did. I guess you couldn't blame her, though, it being her baby daughter and all. The last one to leave the nest is always the hardest to watch fly away. Then, too, they didn't trust their new son-in-law to take care of her out of their sight. They didn't know anything

78

about his background."

"Aunt Annie must have been very much in love with him."

"Oh, that she was, Miss Amy! You could just see the love in her eyes. I rather liked the gentleman she married, myself. I believe he really loved Ann, too."

"Mother said Grandma was used to having her own way all her life. And when Aunt Annie's husband won out about the trip, she caused a scene."

"Missus Margaret was a spoiled southern belle, I'm afraid. When anything didn't go to please her, she'd always cause a scene. Her dramatics started with hand-wringing, graduated to hysterical weeping, and ended in fainting. I can see her now going through the whole ritual the day Ann left! Of course she came out of her faint in time to see Ann and her husband drive out of the yard."

"Aunt Annie must have been made out of different material than Grandma—more durable."

"She was unspoilable. Like her tranquil father. Margaret never understood either one of them. She had no comprehension of love, except self-love. 'What,' she would shout, 'could make a young lady, surrounded by luxury and swathed in security, want to give up such comforts for the raw hardships and toil of the devious West?' 'You'll have no servants out there in the bear-infested woods!' she told Ann. 'Imagine hauling water, and gathering firewood.' But none of her martyr talk changed Ann."

"One has to admire Aunt Annie's spunk."

"The thing that bothered Margaret most was that Ann insisted on leaving most of her fancy wardrobe here. Clothes were Margaret's god. But Ann said she'd have no use for lace and velvet on the frontier. It didn't take

79

things like that to make Ann happy. Margaret's happiness was in her possessions, but, to Ann, life didn't consist of the abundance of her earthly goods. She had different values. That's what baffled Margaret."

"This was Aunt Annie's room, wasn't it?"

"The bed, the chiffonier, the lampstand, the loveseat. . .this is all hers."

"You see why we must find her? Some disposition will have to be made of her things when the property sells."

Amy rummaged through the trunk, finding a small photograph of Ann and one letter written from Ann to her mother. "Aunt Annie was notified when her mother died, wasn't she?"

"Yes, but there was no reply. We supposed they had moved to a new address. I've forgotten now what part of the West they settled in."

Amy studied Ann's picture. "She was a beautiful young lady, wasn't she?"

"I think you favor her."

Amy blushed prettily. "That's quite a compliment; thank you."

"I'm trying to remember when that picture was taken. I'm sure it was before she married."

"Aunt Annie was considerably younger than Mother, wasn't she?"

"Your mother was grown and married before Ann was out of pigtails and pinafores."

"I don't remember Mother talking much about Aunt Annie. Apparently they were not close. The age difference, I guess."

"I don't think your mother approved of Ann's marriage either. She and Margaret had someone else picked out for Ann—a local boy—and she disappointed them both. But I do hope you and Jonathan can find her. I'd be mighty glad to see her again, myself. She was a most gracious child. Will you be going by train or stagecoach?"

"Jonathan says we'll go by coach. It'll take much longer, but that way we can inquire all along and follow any clues we come up with. Most of the stage house hands know the people in their area."

Nina returned to the kitchen and Amy tucked the picture and letter in her pocket. *Aunt Annie's room! Aunt Annie must have loved her husband very much to leave all this behind for an unknown destination with an unknown future. Could I love a man that much?*

Lost in thought, she jumped when Jonathan called her name. He stood in the doorway, grinning boyishly. Amy, as well as all the eligible girls in the township, thought her brother strikingly handsome. "You. . .scared me!" she laughed.

"Are you packed and ready?" he asked.

"Ready, but not quite packed."

"You'll only need a few *simple* outfits for the trip, Amy. We're not going on a pleasure jaunt, you know. And I hope you'll not be trying to impress any wild cowboys— or whip-cracking stagecoach drivers!"

"Jonathan!" Amy shamed, wrinkling her nose comically. "I would never do such an unladylike thing!"

"Never say never," he tormented. "They tell me coach drivers tend to be Romeos."

Amy ignored his teasing, her expression changing to somber. "Jonathan, do you really think we'll find Aunt Annie?"

"If I didn't think so, I wouldn't be making this trip,

81

Sis. Sure, we'll find her!" Jonathan had always been mad-
deningly optimistic in spite of the odds stacked against
him.

"Do you realize that everything in this room belongs
to her? This poster bed. . .the lead glass lamp. . .the chest.
Oh, what if we don't find her? What'll we do with all her
. . .stuff?"

"I won't give up easy, Amy. If she's anywhere to be
found, I'll find her, because she has a right to protest the
sale. We only have a half interest, remember. But if she
cannot be located, we can go ahead with the transaction
and put half the money into a trust fund for her."

"We'll. . .sell her personal items?"

"I'm afraid we'd have to."

"How much luggage are we allowed on the coach?"

"Forty pounds. But if you need more, we'll pay extra."

"I don't see why I'd need anything but my clothes
and toilet articles. How long do you. . .do we. . .expect
to be gone?"

"This trip could run into several months, so don't
short yourself. We have thousands of miles to cover. . .
from here to California. Of course, if we find her right
away. . . ."

"But just think, Jonathan. We'll get to see different
parts of the country and meet lots of new people! I've
always wanted to travel!"

"It'll be a long and tiresome journey. You'll probably
be tired of travel *and* people by the time we get back. My
plans are to go the southern route and return the nor-
thern. I fear the novelty will wear off after a few hot miles.
Are you quite sure you want to go along?"

"Oh, I'm sure! I wouldn't think of letting you go without me. I'm anxious to meet Aunt Annie. And, by the way, I found a picture of her in Grandma's humpback trunk. I thought we ought to take it along." She pulled the photograph from her pocket. "She looks a little bit like Mother, don't you think?"

Jonathan looked at the picture and squinted. "And a *lot* like you."

"Oh, Jonathan! That's what Nina said. But I'm not nearly that pretty."

"Especially your eyes. You didn't happen to find a picture of her notorious husband, did you?"

"Unfortunately, no. Nina says he was about five years older than Auntie and was very charming. Those are the only clues we have on him."

"I wish I could trust my memory as a six-year-old. I recall thinking Ann's fiance was the cleverest gentleman I'd ever seen, with his new wagon and fancy top hat. He tousled my hair and called me Jon-Jon. He was always laughing. I cried to go west with him."

"I was only four when they left. That was seventeen years ago. Do you suppose they went all the way to California?"

"I calculate they did. For gold."

"They could have teenage children by now."

"That's possible, even probable."

"Our cousins. *Cousins*, Jonathan! Doesn't that sound strange?"

"In case Aunt Annie is not living, her part would fall to her children, our cousins."

"Uh-huh."

"Can you be ready to leave by Wednesday, Amy?"

"Yes, dear brother. I'll be ready to meet those cowboys and romantic stagecoach drivers!" Her laughter rippled after him.

Chapter 9

Shipwrecked Heart

"Stage leaves for all points west to Caprock in five minutes. Ladies first, gentlemen." Joseph chanted in a recorded-cylinder tone. The novelty of driving had worn away to perfunctory work, fraught with long days and lonely nights.

Then he saw her. She sat on a bench against the wall, the embodiment of everything he had ever dreamed of, and at his station call she lifted her searching eyes to meet his. They were intense violet eyes with smoky lashes, and he was held by their sweet appeal. The world stopped for Joseph when he gazed into her face. *Where have I seen those eyes before?* he wondered.

A whisper of a dimple threatened her ivory cheeks, sending a thrill through Joseph's muscular frame, cutting his heart loose from its sturdy moorings and setting it afloat. His head swam dizzily and he reached for the door facing for support. She lowered her eyes only after she had shaken his world. He loved her!

His continued stare took in her fresh traveling dress and her perky bonnet doing its best to corral the recalcitrant curls begging escape. She made a picture he would never forget. *If I could capture the heart of a girl like this, I'd gladly throw down the reins,* he told himself honestly. His mother had said the right one would come along, and it looked as if she had just walked into his life. *What has unlocked my heart? Her eyes? Her smile?*

Jim had warned him about stagecoach-riding ladies. And now he had been driving less than two months and it was happening. No girl had ever affected him like this one. *How should I proceed to follow my heart?*

His mouth was open as if to speak, but he had no idea what he had intended to say. He did not know how long he might have remained in his trance-like state, blocking the door and impeding passengers eager for boarding, had not the young man appeared. He was about her age and in his hand he carried a glass of water. He gave her the water, smiling down at her protectively.

She's married! Joseph thought in anguish, and his sailing heart capsized and sunk. He turned and walked resolutely toward the waiting coach.

The Amarillo stop lived up to its reputation as noisy and crowded. "The only thing that makes shadows here is the coach, the people, and the station. . .and maybe a groundhog or two," Jim used to say. But the flat land made for easy traveling and, when a breeze blew from any direction, it was cool if one kept moving.

The coach was filling up. Joseph went over his checklist methodically, glad to be busy. The young man with the girl's suitcase shifted nervously and glanced about. The coach had reached its inside seating capacity.

"Sir," he approached Joseph hesitantly. "I'm Jonathan Browning and this is Amy Browning. I was wondering. . .would it be possible for us to ride on the top with you? The coach is full and we want very much to go farther west today."

"Why. . .yes, certainly," Joseph answered. He wondered how he would manage the miles of her nearness and remonstrated to himself for not considering the possibility that she belonged to someone else. He turned back to the horses.

Jonathan deposited their baggage in the rear and lifted the girl up, placing her between himself and Joseph. When Joseph offered his hand, the dimples threatened to return and he looked away quickly.

"And our driver's name?" Jonathan asked Joseph. Joseph had forgotten to introduce himself.

"I'm Joseph Harris."

"A native of these parts?"

"A native of Texas, yes. But Texas is a vast place. My home is southwest of Fort Worth about fifty miles. A little farming community called Brazos Point on the Brazos River. And you?"

"We live in the eastern part of Kentucky. We've traveled across the country. . .through Nashville, Memphis, Little Rock, Fort Smith, Oklahoma City. . . ."

"Headed for the West Coast?"

"Yes, sir. We're eager to be on our way. We're looking for some relatives that moved West some seventeen years ago. We need their assistance in settling an estate."

"Are you by chance related to the coach house proprietor at Caprock?"

"Not that I know of, sir."

"His name is Browning, too. Mr. David Browning. Wife's name is Grace."

"Could very well be kin," Jonathan mused. "My grandfather, Daniel Browning, had a brother named Zack. Uncle Zack (my great-uncle) had nine boys and they're scattered all over this continent. I don't even know all their names. Mr. David Browning could possibly be one of Uncle Zack's boys."

"That would make him a second cousin," Amy calculated, her voice low and musical. "Wouldn't it be fun to find that we are kin?"

"The Brownings are some of my favorite people," Joseph directed his remarks to Jonathan. "Relatives of mine lived in their area at one time."

"The lady we must find is an aunt on my mother's side of the family," Amy said, but Joseph kept his eyes straight ahead. "We suspect they went all the way to California. She married a man named Andrew or Andrews."

"Lots of people went in search of gold," Joseph supplied, still talking to Jonathan. "An uncle of mine went. . . but never returned. We presume him dead. Murder is a common malady in that lawless country, they say. My uncle's name was Charles Harris. If you happen to run across anyone out there who knows of his whereabouts, my family would be grateful to hear."

"I'll be glad to keep an eye and ear attuned," Jonathan promised.

Amy analyzed their driver with approval. Could Jonathan's teasing about a whip-cracking coach driver have been prophetic? The first time their eyes met, she felt a mutual feeling of admiration, but since then the handsome driver had shut her out of his attention entirely, looking right past her to Jonathan when he spoke. She supposed he was shy.

"My mother and father died almost two years ago in a cholera epidemic," Amy's voice trembled with recent grief. "We have our own home plus Grandfather's place."

The sudden yearning to offer tender sympathies to the sweet lady beside him frightened Joseph. He looked across the miles of sagebrush to purge his mind of her closeness. Miles had never crept by so slowly; the hours turned into individual eternities. It annoyed him—yet it pleased him—that she was involving him in her personal affairs.

"I've never told Jonathan," she gave a shaky lilting laugh, "but I'm anxious to have the estate off our hands because the neighbor is leasing it to grow *tobacco*. You don't smoke do you Mr. . . .Harris?"

"No, ma'am."

"Jonathan doesn't either. And I feel kind of guilty with the sinful stuff growing on the land as long as it belongs to us!"

Jonathan laughed, a deep chuckle. "You never know what to expect from Amy," he volunteered. "She's quite conscientious—almost to a fault."

Joseph wanted to defend her—to say that she was right. But he held his peace.

Some of the passengers disembarked at Tuccumcari to connect with a southbound coach. Amy rode inside the coach the second day, much to Joseph's relief. He saw her only at meal stops and purposely avoided eye contact. But he and Jonathan had struck up a comradeship and

Jonathan rode in the box with Joseph all the way to Caprock. *If I had a wife as delightfully charming as this Jonathan has, I would be with her inside the coach,* Joseph told himself.

"How long have you been driving?" Jonathan asked.

"Nearly two months. I'm new at it. My best friend, Jim Collins, who drove this line for about twelve years, got married and turned the coach to me."

"You and I must be about the same age."

"I'll soon be twenty-two."

"I've just turned twenty-three and Amy is twenty-one."

Amy. . .what a beautiful name.

"Do you plan to go all the way to California by coach?"

"No, I thought I'd take the train over the mountains and across the desert."

"There's a train with connections at Lamy, sixteen miles from Santa Fe, that'll take you all the way to Los Angeles. I'll be going to Sante Fe on some land business after a short layover at Caprock. Be glad to offer you transportation." Joseph forgot that the package deal would include Amy. Too late he remembered. He'd given his word.

"I'd be much obliged, Mr. . . . ."

"You can just call me Joseph."

"Joseph."

Joseph swung the coach about to a prize stop at the Caprock station. Grace Browning greeted him with a motherly hug. He waited for the passengers to unload their luggage before turning the horses into the lot. Then he returned to make introductions, anxious to know if the two sets of Brownings would discover any bonds of

90

kinship.

"I'm from a large family of Brownings scattered all over the west," Mr. Browning told Jonathan. "My family came this direction when I was a small lad. My father's name was Zachary Browning, but they called him Zack. My mother's name was Charlotte."

Amy's violet eyes danced as she laid her dainty hand on Jonathan's arm. "Oh, how nice!" she murmured, her excitement evident.

"You don't say! Zack Browning was my great-uncle," Jonathan gripped David Browning's hand in a steel-grip handshake. "My grandfather was Daniel Browning, Zack Browning's brother. It looks as though we've found some of our long lost kinfold."

"Second cousins!" Grace Browning beamed. A happy babble of talk ensued.

Joseph feined weariness and begged to be excused while the newly found relatives visited. "It's been a long day and I'm still tense behind the team," he said. But to himself he added *"Plus I fell and bruised my heart."*

"Wait, Joseph. You have some mail." Grace Browning handed Joseph Dessie's letter. "I'm not meaning to be personal, but I'd like to know that there's no bad news from your family before you retire."

Amy stole a secret look at the fine lines of Joseph's face. *No fickle Romeo, this one.*

He scanned the letter quickly. "Everything's fine in the physical sense," he explained, "but my younger brothers and sisters think it's terrible. They lost their schoolteacher and haven't been able to find a replacement. They asked me to keep a lookout for someone who might be interested in the job along the coach line. I have little

91

hopes of finding such a person. Effie's heart is set on going to school this fall. With her disability, it'll depend on the teacher they get, of course.''

"Thank you, Joseph. That relieves my worries.''

Joseph took his letter along with his shipwrecked heart to his room to suffer alone, while a new plan, hardly perceptible at first, took shape in Amy's mind.

It was a ridiculous plan, but perhaps it would work!

Chapter 10

Amy's Decision

"*A*ny news you want to send to Jim and Charlotte, Mrs. Browning?"

"You'll be going on to Sante Fe?"

"I'm making a business trip to see about Charles's land."

"If it wouldn't be any bother, I'll send a letter by you to Charlotte. And I've some mesquite bean jelly I've put up for Jim if you have room to take it. It's his favorite."

"Plenty of room. There'll just be me and Jonathan and Amy." He had not meant to say her name; it rolled from his tongue unbidden. His ears burned red.

"Oh, hasn't Amy told you? She has decided to stay with me and Dave for awhile and let Jonathan pursue the chase at his leisure. Dave and I are delighted!" Grace Browning's eyes were bright. House guests were her greatest pleasure. "You'll be coming back through soon, won't you?"

"In about a week." *Is Amy ill? Will she join her hus-band in California later when she is better able to travel? Why would a husband leave a wife so young and vulner-able? But what business is it of mine? I should rejoice that I will soon be out of the field of her attraction rather than question the reasons for the curtailment of her travels.*

The dust from the coach wheels had scarcely settled when Amy asked, "The coach driver. . .Mr. Harris. . . Joseph. . .he's not married, is he?"

Grace Browning chuckled. "Oh my goodness, no! A mighty good catch he'll be for some young lady, too! Those kind are few and far between nowadays. Made out of raw-hide and eiderdown!"

"But he seems so. . .inaccessible. Is he like this with all girls?"

"All of them so far. My own daughter, Charlotte, set her sights on him three years ago when Jim Collins brought him to visit The Territory. With all her feminine charms working overtime, she didn't get from Dan to Beersheba with him. Of course, it was just an infatuation with her. She found her heartthrob and married him two months ago. He was Joseph's best friend."

"Was he a stage driver?"

"He was a stage driver."

"Yes, I remember now that Mr. Harris. . .uh, Joseph mentioned the former driver's recent wedding."

"How do you feel about this stage driver?"

Amy laughed. "Before we left home, Jonathan teased me about making eyes at cowboys or stage drivers. I vowed it would never happen. Mr. Harris. . .Joseph. . .is one driver I wouldn't mind making eyes at!"

"If you can even get him to look at you?"

Amy gave a little sigh. "That's the problem. The first time I saw him, giving the stage call in Amarillo, he looked directly at me and I felt. . .sensed. . .an interest on his part. It was as if. . .just for a little moment. . .our hearts communed. Then he looked away and it vanished. Just like that. In spite of my best efforts, I haven't been able to revive it. I don't mind admitting, I am smitten! Do you suppose the feeling. . .frightened Joseph?"

"I don't see why it should have. Up until last year, Joseph had some worrisome family problems that hindered him from giving consideration to his own future. He put his family first, though I never thought it was quite fair to him. But now he has things pretty well ironed out at home. So don't be discouraged. Now would be a good time to capture his heart. There's a vacancy there."

"That's good news."

"If the interest was there once, it'll likely return."

"Mrs. Browning. . .I've got a plan. . .it may seem like a very foolish plan to you. But I've been thinking about it and praying about it ever since last night. I talked with Jonathan and he said the decision is mine since I'm of age. . . ."

"What's that, dear?"

"While Jonathan is scouting the continent for Aunt Annie, I would like very much to take that school-teaching job in Joseph's home community until they can find a replacement. Until Christmas, maybe. I would be near his family and could learn more about Joseph. He said there was a child who needed special attention."

"An afflicted family member. He's very protective of her."

"I gathered that."

"The pay wouldn't likely be very good."

"I don't need money."

Grace Browning raised her eyebrows knowingly. "But you do need a chance to see Joseph now and then."

"You're very perceptive, Mrs. Browning. I would welcome the opportunity."

"Then, by all means, take the teaching job. It'll be a challenging adventure."

Meanwhile, Joseph and Jonathan hastened westward. "I'm glad Amy stayed," Jonathan said matter-of-factly. "She loves the Brownings and their part of the country already. California is a pretty tough place, I hear, and I won't have to worry about her safety at Caprock. I can move about faster without being concerned for her welfare. I tried to talk her into staying home, but she *would* come with me."

Strange way to feel about one's wife. This statement was to himself, then aloud Joseph asked, "How long will you spend searching for her aunt?"

Her aunt? puzzled Jonathan. Then he replied, "It may take weeks—and it may take months. Time really isn't important. . .just so I'm successful."

"Small talk often leads to a big friendship," Jim had said once, and when Jonathan extended a hand for a hearty handshake at the Lamy station, Joseph knew that proverb had been fulfilled between himself and Jonathan. "We'll meet again when my manhunt is over," Jonathan assured. "Make sure Amy behaves herself in my absence!" And he was gone.

When the engine chugged out of sight around the mountains, Joseph hastened toward Cristo Haven, eager to see Jim and Charlotte, trying to sort his thoughts as he went. *Amy certainly didn't seem like the sort of wife given to misbehaving. What had Jonathan meant. . ."Make sure Amy behaves herself"? A joke, no doubt.*

Lilly explained in her lame English that Jim and Charlotte were out and would return presently. "Sit?" she motioned, all happiness at seeing the family friend.

Joseph welcomed the opportunity to meditate. Signs of love and home surrounded him. Charlotte's knitting basket lay beside a soft chair, brilliantly colored threads forming an afghan. In another settee nearby, Jim's book lay face down, marking his place. The feeling that he might be missing life's choicest riches weighed heavy on the scales of Joseph's priorities as he indulged in reflection. He had to admit to himself that driving the coach was much less fulfilling than he had anticipated. Repetitious scenery and long, lonely hours made him wonder if, indeed, he was as "cut out" for the work as he had hoped.

"Joseph!" Jim pounded him on the back. "Don't tell me you've brought the coach back already?"

Joseph grinned. "Actually I came on business. . .to try to secure my land."

Charlotte followed her husband, flushed and glowing, "Why, what a pleasant surprise, Joseph Harris!" she said. Joseph handed her the letter that Grace Browning had sent, then turned to Jim. "You haven't been left out," he teased. "Your doting mother-in-law sent you some jelly."

"The best mother-in-law in the world," Jim crowed. "How's business?"

"Heavy. I expect, though, it'll slack off after the summer run."

"Generally does. How's driving treating you?"

"Brutal. I met a lady back at the Amarillo stop that I'd have thrown down any set of reins for. Right then and there."

"I can't believe it!" squealed Charlotte. "Joseph smitten!"

"I warned you, Joseph!" reminded Jim. "Those stage-riding ladies are wily."

"That's not all the story." Talking about it unburdened Joseph's mind. He had to tell somebody. Charlotte leaned forward to listen. "This has an O. Henry ending. Just when I thought I'd met the woman of my dreams, up walked her *husband*!"

"Aw," Charlotte consoled, sliding back into her chair. "What a letdown. I don't like stories that end like that, Joseph Harris!"

"Well, the whole thing is ironic. Guess who she was?" He let the suspense mount to a crescendo.

"We wouldn't know her, of course."

"Your cousin's wife, Charlotte."

"*My* cousin's wife?"

"Your third cousin. Man named Jonathan Browning. Prettiest little wife I ever laid eyes on—sparkling violet eyes, all innocence and heart-fetching—named Amy."

Jim groaned. "Your luck, Joseph!"

"I'll never find another one like her."

"Don't be so fatalistic," begged Charlotte. "The world's a big place with lots of pretty girls. How did you find out he was *my* cousin?"

"I brought them to Caprock. He got to talking with your father and discovered that his grandfather and yours were brothers."

"Where were they from?"

"Back in Kentucky somewhere."

"And what brought them to Caprock?"

"They started west looking for some lost aunt of hers to settle up an estate left to her by her grandfather. She's apparently pretty well fixed."

"Ah, yes, money talks."

"I would have felt the same had she been penniless."

"They went on to California?"

"He did. I brought him to the Lamy depot and put him on the train for Los Angeles today. She stayed in Caprock."

"He left his wife at *Mother's*?" Charlotte asked.

"Yes. Said he was glad to leave her so he could go on without worrying about her safety."

"Then he'll be returning soon?"

"Said it might be months."

"This doesn't add up, Joseph. His wife will spend the whole time with Mother?"

"I don't know what this wife of his is going to do," Joseph's voice was almost impatient. "And I don't care. I just found my ideal. . .and lost her all in five minutes. . . and now I'll go through life trying to find the likes of her . . .and probably not succeeding. It's not fair." He sighed heavily.

"No, it's not," agreed Charlotte.

"How's the family, Joseph? And Effie?" Jim questioned.

Joseph launched into a detailed reply, thankful for the change of subject. "Not much rain in Central Texas this year. The well's gone dry, Dessie says. But they live close to water, so that's no big deal. Their school teacher, Miss Vivian, gave notice of her resignation and they've not found anyone to take her place. They wrote wanting me to inquire along the line for a teacher. You don't have any spare teachers seeking a change of scenery from gorgeous snow-capped mountains to dry, barren farmlands and a cut in salary, do you?"

"You won't get one with that kind of sales talk," Jim laughed.

"Effie had her heart set on going to school this fall, and Miss Vivian had promised to take her and give her the special help she needs. Miss Vivian was a patient sort, mothering all her pupils. But now I suppose it'll depend on the teacher they get—if they get one at all—whether or not Effie will be accepted. Not just any teacher would be understanding."

"We'll adopt her and send her to school, won't we, Jim?"

"Any minute she's put up for adoption, we get first claim," Jim responded. "And by the way, do you know what we're going to name our firstborn son, Joseph?"

"I'd never guess."

"Joseph."

"I'd be honored. And do you know what I'm going to name my firstborn daughter?" Joseph jested.

"Amy!"

"How did you ever guess?"

Chapter 11

New Family, New Troubles

"*A* new fam'ly by th' name o' Grimes moved in over at th' old Robbins place on th' river." Henry stood with his hands burrowed in the pockets of his baggy overalls, watching Martha skim the milk.

"I thought th' flood washed th' old Robbins house away."

"It did, but a part o' th' barn still stands in th' upper field an' they're livin' in that. Leaks like a sieve."

"How shameful. Th' poor souls."

"They don't seem to mind none a tall."

"Bought th' place, I 'spect?"

"Jest rentin', I think. Don't look plush enough to buy nuthin'."

"Bro. Stevens'll be glad to get some new faces at church."

"Mr. Grimes told me right off they warn't churchgoin'

people."

"Well, it becomes our duty to be neighborly to 'um an' mayhap win 'um to th' Lord."

"Mr. Grimes said he shore hoped th' people here was friendlier than where they moved from. Said they really had lousy neighbors, always meddlin' an' mistreatin' 'um an' all."

"Have they got any kids?"

"Two teenagers. A boy that looks bout seventeenish an' a girl a couple o' years er so younger. He said they hadn't been able to find no good schools fer their kids nowhere they been. They've moved from place to place pretty reg'lar tryin' to find a decent school."

"Did you tell 'um we got th' very best in th' country? That is, if'n we can find a teacher by commencin' time."

"Yep. I told 'im that th' neighbors 'n school was fine in our little community. We ain't never had no complaints from nobody what ever lived here."

"But Henry, it's a powerful bad year to start in farmin' in these here parts with this drought an' all. An' they're too late to start crops even if'n they wouldn't burn up."

"He says he ain't no farmer. . .that he ain't never farmed in 'is life an' don't 'spect to start now."

"Then what does he think on doin' fer a livin' 'round here?"

"That warn't none of my business to ask, Martha. Wouldn't want 'im to think right off we was nosy neighbors pryin' into his personal affairs!"

Trouble cropped up without delay. William came home from the creek fighting mad. "Mama!" he seethed. "That new boy named Claude Grimes got my catfish off'n my trotline! It was th' big yellow cat I've been tryin' to snag all summer long. Must a weighed twenty pounds er more. I jest happened to walk up on Claude runnin' my line!"

"Why didn't ye explain to 'im that it was your'n?"

"I did. I tried to take it away from 'im. But he jest laughed real loud at me an' said this was a free river an' th' fish warn't fer nobody in partic'lar. He said he was an American same as we was, an' 'twas finders keepers, losers weepers."

"Did you tell 'im 'twas your hooks an' line what caught th' fish an' you put it out an' baited it an'. . . ."

"Yes'm. He laughed all th' harder an' said he didn't get my hooks ner my line ner nothin' that belonged to me. He said if'n I didn't shut my trap an' keep it shut, he'd throw me in th' river an' drown me headfirst."

Martha shuddered. This kind of idle talk frightened her. "That big fish shore would'a made us a feast, all right, but mayhap they needed it worse'n us, William," she sighed.

"But it's th' principle o' it, Mama. They may need it bad, but 'tain't right!"

"No. 'Tain't right, William. It's stealin'."

Some time later, Claude showed up at the Harris's door and asked to borrow half a sack of mash. "Maw needs it," he told Martha.

"I knowed you'd want me to help th' poor people out," she said to Henry that night. "Th' Bible says to share. If'n it was us in th' same need, we'd want. . . ."

"But Martha," Henry interrupted. "They don't have no chickens! They don't have no animals, 'cept a scroungy, flea-bitten dog. An' dogs don't eat mash."

That week, Martha baked a double-crust pie, using her scarce and precious commodities, sacrificially taking

103

it to her new neighbor. "Watch Sally whiles I take this pie to th' new Grimes family," she instructed Dessie, wiping her hands on her faded apron.

Then she took herself to the sagging barn on the old Robbins place. "We want to welcome you here," she told the scowling Mrs. Grimes. "You've come to a mighty pleasant neighborhood. I baked this here pie for yore family. I figgered it'd be awhile afore you could get yer stove goin' an' all." The smell of rotting fruit made her feel queasy.

"We don't want no charity from nobody an' we don't want to be obliged to nobody," Mrs. Grimes retorted, still frowning. "An' furthermore, Jake don't like nobody comin' 'round our place."

"Beggin' pardon, but we wanted to offer our neighborliness with no offenses meant an' 'spectin' no returns. An' we'd like to invite you to our church, too. We have a mighty fine parson."

"Jake don't believe in no God. Maw made me go to church when I was a kid an' there warn't nobody went there 'cept simperin' hypocrites. I ain't been to church since I growed up an' married Jake, an' I ain't makin' no plans on startin' now."

"But yer two children. . . ."

"I shore ain't makin' my children go to nobody's church like my Maw did me. It ruint me on religion. I don't believe in forcin' salvation on kids. I used to send 'um sometime but got to where folks wadn't friendly to 'um. I never yet seen a church that showed no true kindness. All o' 'um is out fer th' tithe money. That's all they care 'bout."

"Oh, Brother Stevens ain't that way a tall. He. . . ."

"Tell yer preacher man to not be comin' 'round, cause

he shore won't be welcome. Jake'd probably shoot 'im fer trespassin' without battin' an eye." Mrs. Grimes took a can from her filthy apron pocket and spat vehemently into it.

Martha still held the pie in her hand. Mrs. Grimes looked at it scornfully. She showed her teeth stained with snuff, but it wasn't a smile. It rather reminded Martha of a grimace the devil might give. "Take yer pie back home with yer. I don't want Jake to know anybody's been here on this property. He'd ask who, an' it would be bad fer ye. Now git."

A perturbed Martha took herself home. "Henry, our new neighbors spell trouble."

"I'm afeared so, Martha. An' one bad apple can spoil a whole community."

"I felt th' devil over there when I went to take them a pie, Henry. An' you know what? She refused th' pie. An' she said if'n Pastor Stevens tried to visit, her husband would be prone to shoot 'im dead!"

"We'd best warn th' parson."

Chester burst in the front door aghast. "Mama!" he sputtered, his eyes dilated. "Th' new girl from over at th' Robbins place wears her brother's overalls an' *swaggers* when she walks. She don't spit white, neither. She's a tomboy!"

"She cusses, too," William added dryly. "An' whistles at all th' boys."

"You know what her name is?" Dessie supplied. "It's *Sonny!* Can you imagine a girl's name being *Sonny?*"

"That's bound not to be 'er real name," Martha said. "That's a boy's name."

"She says if'n we know what's good fer us, that's

105

what we'd best call 'er an' leave off sissy names."

"Sonny said she thought Pauline Stevens was the stuck-upest girl she'd ever seen in 'er life," Dessie continued her report, "but she thinks Matthew's kinda cute. She said she'd like to bust 'um up!"

"They sure do a lot of braggin'," William complained. "Claude brags all time."

"Children, I don't like us to get in th' habit o' talkin' 'bout people," Martha warned, "even if they're not respectable. I think th' best thing all o' you can do is keep yer distance from them till they prove to be fittin' fer our association."

"Well, it's th' truth, Mama," William defended, pursuing his story. "Claude 'specially brags about what his Paw can do. 'Paw can do this, Paw can do that.' I'm sick o' hearin' what his Paw can do." Henry entered the room and stood listening.

"An' I know fer sure Claude tells lies, 'cause he said th' last place they lived that his paw made th' *moon shine!* I told 'im that he was crazy, cause only God could make th' moon shine. He laughed till he most nigh cried!"

"Moonshine!" Henry looked at Martha agog. "I knowed somethin' warn't right from th' first day they moved here. There's muscadine an' winter grapevines all over th' ole Robbins place. An' water from th' creek. Yep. Moonshine, all right. Don't be lettin' 'um have no more mash, Martha. He ain't usin' it fer th' right purpose. *Moonshine!* Our troubles is jest begun."

Chapter 12

Jonathan's Discovery

"*T*his establishment has housed many a prospector," Mrs. Bimski proclaimed proudly to Jonathan, who took a room in the large, remodeled hotel. "Some stayed a night, others a week or a year. I have the register of every guest back to 1870."

"That bit of information pleases me," Jonathan returned, appraising the proprietor with one swift glance. She was middle-aged and maternal, a genteel soul upon whom the hardness of the West had not been able to lay its curse. She and Amy would have gotten along well together.

"You're out here prospecting, too?"

"No, Ma'am. I've come in search of some relatives whom we believe came for the gold. They left eastern Kentucky in 1872 or 1873 the best we can calculate. We've lost track of them."

"When was the last time you heard from them?"

"It's been more than ten years ago. We don't even have a previous address."

"Their name?"

"Ann and Charles Andrew or Andrews. We're not positive on that last name. Finding them is going to be a challenge with no more particulars than we have."

"I'm afraid it will. Especially with the mob of people that have been in and out of the state since the gold was discovered. You've come all the way from Kentucky to look for them in person?"

"Yes, ma'am."

"You must have a special message for them to travel this far searching."

"I do. We're trying to settle up an estate. Ann Andrews is an heir and we need her signature on the papers. Besides, she has some personal belongings that she left behind."

"I see. Well, I'll help you all I can, Mr. Browning. You can go through my register and see what you can find. I boast a rather good memory of people myself, and I don't recall an Ann Andrews. Did they have any children?"

"We have no idea how many. We have one letter in our possession. Aunt Ann announced that she was in a family way in that letter. So there must be at least one."

"You might check birth and death notices at the Courthouse. They weren't all recorded over the years, especially way back, but a good many of them were."

"Thank you. That's a good suggestion."

"And make yourself at home while you're here, Mr. Browning. If I can do anything for your comfort, you're to let me know."

"Yes, ma'am."

Fruit trees laden with blossoms, date palms, olive trees, and the fresh salt air made Jonathan wish for Amy. Had he known that he would find such a pleasant lodging, he would have insisted on her coming. She would have been company for him now.

He knew she would want a detailed description of the terrain. She was like that—wanting explicit detail. He tried to think of how he could put into words the panorama of wide sandy beaches reaching out to the peaceful blue-green ocean. "The Wild West has its tame ocean," he would tell her, "contrasting with the tame East's wild ocean." Poetry wasn't his talent; his phrases always turned out prosaic.

It still surprised him to think that Amy chose to stay behind. He tried to imagine what precipitated her whimsical decision to answer the Macedonian call to teach school in the small community in drought striken Central Texas. Jonathan suspected that it had something to do with Joseph Harris, and the thought pleased him. Coach driver though he was, Joseph was no whip-cracking, run-of-the-mill driver. He was, in fact, one of the few that would be worthy of Amy.

Jonathan settled into his modernly refurbished room, took Ann's picture from his traveling valise, and started his long search. He spent the days in reviewing city records and the evenings in pouring over the hotel registry by lamplight. Guests' names were listed with their former residences and dates of arrival. Jonathan started with the 1872 book, carefully examining each entry. When he had found no Andrews listed through 1877, he entertained growing doubts that they had ever lodged here, but refused to give up his search until he had thoroughly scanned every page of every book.

It was after a tiresome day in town that he picked up the 1878 book and continued turning pages far into the night. Eyes weary with strain and head beginning to ache as name after name marched before his blurring vision, Jonathan suddenly stopped short. Here, listed under December, 1878, Jonathan found the neatly penned name of Charles Harris with a notation "From Caprock, Territory of New Mexico." He caught his breath in disbelief! He had located Joseph's uncle!

Excitement forbade sleep. Before daylight, he questioned Mrs. Bimski in the kitchen where she laid out the yeast bread to rise for the morning meal. (It was no wonder that her boardinghouse was filled to capacity!) "I found a Charles Harris in the 1878 registry."

"I thought you said Charles Andrews."

"I did, but. . . ."

"Charles Harris was a relative of yours, too?"

"No, ma'am. He's the uncle of a mutual friend of mine. Is he still living here?"

"No, but I remember Charles Harris well. He boarded here with us for over a year. Many mornings he got up before my other roomers and sat right there where you're sitting while I rolled out the bread, and talked to me. A marvelous personality and extremely handsome. Lonely, though."

"He didn't have a family here?"

"He was a widower. His wife, Rebecca, died back at Caprock of consumption or something. He talked of her incessantly and also of his 'little angel' as he called her—a

110

child he left behind with relatives in Texas. I knew his heartbreak, for I had lost my husband, too."

"The nephew I mentioned is from Texas."

"I wonder if it was part of the same family. Charles made good and gave notice that he'd be returning to his 'angel' in a fortnight. I believe he told me he posted a letter to the relatives stating such. I was dreading to see him leave, but mighty glad for his sake. New light came in his eyes and he was happier than I'd ever seen him before. He never saw the day he dreamed of, unfortunately. He was killed."

"Killed?"

"Shot outright. It wasn't the first one I'd had from my hotel that had been killed, but I never get used to senseless murders. With Charles Harris, it was. . .a deeper hurt. I've always wondered if he was mistaken for someone else. Nobody could have hated Charles. Why, everybody loved him! It's possible, of course, that somebody wanted his fortune. But he had no money on his person when he met his fate. No, I think somebody just got the wrong person."

"He left his earnings to his. . .angel?"

"We never learned what he did with his fortune. I checked with the local banks, seeking funds for his burial. None of them handled his account. These prospectors— you never know where they keep their holdings. He may have had the gold buried or hidden. Who knows? I arranged for his funeral myself."

"That was kind of you."

"I grieved for years that I did not have the address of those relatives in Texas with whom his 'angel' lived. It was stupid of me not to get an address, knowing what

111

can happen here. But surely they've surmised the truth by now."

"It's what Joseph, the nephew, feared. It's a fear of all the homefolks when a loved one comes west."

"Since that incident, I try to obtain addresses of next of kin—especially of the prospectors."

"I'll be in contact with Joseph and will pass on the unfortunate information to him."

"You'll be seeing some of Charles's relatives?"

"That's my plan. After my own search is complete."

"Among his scant belongings were two papers. One was his marriage license and the other was a paper on some land he had been living on. I've had them in safekeeping, hoping some relative would eventually be located. One never wants to destroy valuable documents. They don't take up much storage room. The other items— clothing and boots—I took to the charity barrel. Would you be so kind as to take these papers to the nephew?"

"I'd be glad to. And. . .is Charles buried near here somewhere?"

"Right here in the city cemetery, northeast section. I put up a small marker. Wish I could have done more. I found his date of birth listed on his marriage certificate. Charles was much too special to sleep in an unmarked pauper's grave with no mourners."

"I'd like to visit the grave before I leave."

"It's but half a mile south of here. Easy walking distance. Take a flower from a pot on the front veranda and lay it on the mound for me."

"And I'll be glad to pay you back any expense."

Mrs. Bimski waved the idea away with her hand. "Oh, no, I wouldn't think of it. If it had been one of my own

112

in a 'foreign land,' I would have wanted someone to bury mine honorably. The good Lord's already paid me back a hundredfold since that day."

After breakfast, Jonathan visited the hedge-encased graveyard. Walking through the burial grounds past rows of symmetrical mounds, he read headstones that bore tender epitaphs. He wondered how many had lost their lives to gain a corruptible crown of riches. He knew Joseph would be proud of the peaceful cemetery where his uncle rested, and the relaying of Mrs. Bimski's kindnesses would bring a measure of comfort.

When he found Charles Harris' headstone—a nice marble one—he knelt respectfully to read the inscription: "Charles Harris, Born May 13, 1850—Died March 31, 1880." Chipped into the stone was this short message: "To live in the lives of those we leave behind is not to die."

Whatever the future days revealed or withheld, the discovery of Joseph's uncle had made Jonathan's journey worth the effort. Surely, he felt, fate had smiled upon him to send him to Mrs. Bimski's boarding house. Now he must resume his search for Ann.

The next morning, he took Ann's daguerreotype to Mrs. Bimski. "This is Aunt Ann's likeness before she was married. You would perhaps remember a tenant this beautiful?"

"Yes, a face that pretty I would remember." Mrs. Bimski combed her memory for the face. "No, Mr. Browning, I don't believe that lady ever lodged here," she said. "Not even for a night."

Chapter 13

The Oldtimer's Story

"*H*ow's your day, laddie?"

The oldtimer sat on the portico, with his chair leaned on its two back legs and his black high-topped shoes propped on the porch railing, stroking the crook of his cane. Jonathan guessed him to be seventy-five, but with the arduous, fast living of the West it was hard to tell.

When Mr. Sawyer asked a question—even as innocent as "How's your day?"—he didn't want an answer, he wanted an audience. The garrulous tenant bragged of being the senior resident of the hotel, and Jonathan suspected he stayed on because he had a glad eye for Mrs. Bimski. He noted that Mrs. Bimski had patiently resigned herself to Mr. Sawyer's harmless overtures, giving him an occasional patronizing pat on the shoulder much as she would give a small child. This slight gesture of affection satisfied the old fellow's egotistical yearnings for attention.

Jonathan tried to escape the oldtimer's harangue for the most part, but today he was desperate for information, whatever its source.

"Fine, thank you," Jonathan answered Mr. Sawyer's question. "I was wondering. . . ."

"Yep. I said I almost beat the forty-niners here," he boasted to Jonathan. "I was a young man living in Oklahoma. A sawed-off place called Okmulgee. Indian name town with lots of Cherokees there. You know that's the tribe that was deported by the government. Chief John Ross was their leader. I seen him personally. Lots of them died in the deportation. It was a pity, I said, a crying pity. . . ."

"Did you ever. . . ?"

"Lots of Indian-named towns in Oklahoma. . . Okemah, Talequah—the Cherokee's capital—Okfuskee, Muskogee. . . . Anyway, I said, 'Sawyer, you're an Okie fool to sit here digging in the coal pits of Oklahoma when you could be in California digging for pure gold,' I said."

"You met a lot of early prospectors, I suppose?"

"*Thousands* of them. I was on the Barbary Coast for more than a year during the population explosion. Whew, it was something! I said, 'This bawdy, lawless coast, I'm getting out of here' I said. Lots of violence. Forty thousand people came in two years. Can you imagine? *Forty thousand people!* Now, I'm a peaceful man. I said, 'I'm finding me a quieter place to live,' I said. Sutter's Mill was literally overrun with people. All kinds of people. Good, bad, and middlin'. People from everywhere. I don't believe there was a state or province that wasn't represented. I said, 'I'm going to Los Angeles,' I said. Would

116

you believe it, Mr. . . ."

"Jonathan Browning."

"Laddie, that I was here when California became a state in 1850?"

Jonathan found it difficult to thread a word in anywhere. He could only hope that the oldtimer would run down by and by.

"Never seen a state have such a hard time deciding on a capital. First they chose San Jose. That would have been all right with me, but I guess they weren't satisfied with it, so they changed to Monterey. Still didn't please them, so they moved lock, stock, and barrel to Vallejo. I said, 'I wish they'd make up their minds and quit being so changeable,' I said. They finally settled on Sacramento in '54."

"Did you ever meet up with anyone by the name of . . . ?"

Mr. Sawyer appeared not to hear Jonathan. "Railroad came through here in 1869 connecting us all the way to the other side of the continent. I said, 'This is going to make a big difference,' I said. 'We'll get piled up here like a cattle stampede,' I said. Before that we had to depend on ships, stagecoaches, pony express, and the telegraph. 'Now with them steam engines, things are fixing to pep up,' I said."

Mr. Sawyer tapped his cane against a rung on the chair and continued importantly, " 'Yep,' I said, 'this railroad's gonna make a lot of difference for California,' I said. And bless me, it did! Brought a whole new wave of immigration. By then things was getting mighty crowded. Then the big ranchos started. The first trainload of oranges was shipped out of this very town we're sitting in back in 1886. I said, 'We're just beginning to boom,' I said. Strange, though, I had no hankering to go back to Oklahoma. I guess I'd got used to the shoving and elbowing."

"I came out here looking for. . . ." Jonathan tried again, but Mr. Sawyer was lost in his own reverie.

"Not everybody that came out here struck it rich. I didn't do so bad myself, but I seen many a poor beggar look for a pot of gold and didn't even find the rainbow. Nope, didn't find it. Rainbows vanished before their eyes. I said, 'There's gonna be a lot of disappointed people,' I said. And a lot of people lost their lives, too. That's the bad part."

"Did you know Charles Harris?" Jonathan said it fast, and the oldtimer was immediately sidetracked by the familiar name.

"Charles Harris? Did you say Charles Harris? Why, yes! Charles lived right here in this very hotel. Roomed next to me. I said, 'That's one of the finest gentlemen I ever knowed,' I said. Never drank a drop of alcohol, showed a good Samaritan spirit, and I can tell you one thing, laddie—he lived his religion. And that's more than you could say for the bulk of them. Most everybody left their religion back home if they ever had any to start with. Charles trusted everybody too much, though. I said, 'He's too good for this roaring disorder,' I said. 'He needs to go back home where he came from.' I said, 'I wish he'd get out of here while the gettin's good,' I said."

"I'm a friend of his nephew. He brought me partway by coach."

"If the nephew's anything like Charles Harris, he'll do you proud for a friend, Mr. . . . ."

118

"Browning."

"Oh, yes, laddie. Charles always seemed lonely, though. I said, 'He's missing his family,' I said. Course he told me all about how his pretty little wife died and left him with a sickly child. He worried all the time about that child."

Mr. Sawyer adjusted his spectacles and stroked his white beard. "I said, 'She's probably in good care,' I said, trying to cheer him up. And he said he had taken her to relatives in Texas and he was afraid his sister-in-law was prejudiced against her and he needed to make his fortune and hurry back to her. I said, 'He's just working too hard,' I said. He got thin and haggard looking. 'He's not getting enough rest,' I said. Then one day he came up dead, an everyday tragedy of this wild country back then. I said, 'I sure wish he'da got out a little sooner,' I said. He lost it all. Made old Sawyer want to cry. Yep, made old Sawyer want to cry."

"Mrs. Bimski told me where Charles was buried and I visited his grave yesterday."

"I went to his funeral, him being my next door neighbor and good friend. Nicest little service I ever attended. Preacher said if all prospectors was as honest and clean as this one was, wouldn't be no lawlessness and feuding. I said, 'That preacher's got Charles pegged right,' I said. I said, 'His family can't be here to do the honors, so I'll stand in for them,' I said."

"Thank you for telling me about Charles Harris. Now I'm looking for. . . ."

"I'm glad you found a relative for Charles. Miz Bimski about worried herself sick because she had no addresses to notify the next of kin. That's just like Miz Bimski to fret over her tenants. There ain't a kinder lady in this whole state than Miz Bimski."

"I'm sure there's not."

"There was a lot of loose girls around here back when Charles took lodging, and some of them set their sights on Charles Harris. But Charles told me that once he knowed his Rebecca, there'd never be another lady ever take her place. I said, 'She must have been a mighty special gal,' I said."

"A Mr. Andrews."

"Mr. who?"

"I'm looking for a Mr. Andrews. Have you met anyone by that name. It's very important that I find him."

"Andrews. . .Andrews. . .Yes, I met a Carl Andrews back in the late 70's. Have you ever been in a prospector's shack, laddie? They're the shoddiest, grimiest hovels you ever saw. I said, 'That fighting burly man will survive out here,' I said. 'He can outdrink, outswear, and outlive all of 'em,' I said." The oldtimer slapped his knee, proud of his cleverness.

At last, a clue! "Was he. . .did he have a wife?"

"I 'spect he did, laddie, but it didn't keep his eye from roving. He didn't have her with him—fortunately or unfortunately—but he had a picture on the wall of his shanty of some little boy with thick, straw-colored hair and freckles. Called him Junior. I said, 'Must be married,' I said."

"You wouldn't happen to know the name of his. . . wife? Was it Ann?"

"Never heard him mention his wife's name. Just called her his 'old lady.' I said, 'He's not a very respectful sort,' I said." Sawyer stopped abruptly, as if he realized he had already said too much. "He's not. . .a relative of

120

yours, is he?"

"If he is, he'd be an in-law. No blood relation. He may be my lost uncle by marriage."

"Then I'd advise you to just leave him lost, laddie," Sawyer chuckled at his own joke. "No offense about your relatives, but the truth stands firm on two stout legs, I always said."

"Carl might be short for Charles."

"Might be. I wouldn't know. All I ever heard was Carl."

"You think this Carl Andrews is still living?"

"Oh, I expect so. Tough as nails. Nothing short of lightning from heaven could kill him, I said."

"Would he still be in the mining shacks in California?"

"No, he didn't stay long. Maybe six or eight months. Whipped up on everything and everybody while he was here, though, and left with his share of the loot. Them's the kind that survive out here—the bad kind—while the good ones like Charles Harris gets picked off. Old Carl said he was going to the Oregon Territory. I expect that's where he'd left his wife and son. I said, 'That's one thing he did smart—take his money and git,' I said."

"You wouldn't have any idea what part of Oregon he lives in, I don't suppose?"

"Around Portland somewhere. Ain't heared from him since he left and, to be truthful, I ain't hankerin' to."

"Can you describe to me what he looked like?"

"Well, he was tall and rawboned. Had a red face and a large nose from drinking too much liquor. . .and a pot belly. His hair was straw-colored, just a bit darker than the picture of the little boy on the wall. His eyes were the color of. . . ." Mr. Sawyer chopped his sentence off

121

abruptly. "For honest, you're not going to try to *find* the good-for-nothing, are you?"

"I'm afraid I must. If he is the man married to my aunt, I must find them to settle an estate back in Kentucky. Aunt Ann left many of her personal belongings behind."

"If your aunt is married to Carl Andrews, you might need to find her and rescue her from the devil."

Jonathan wasted no time in booking passage for the Oregon Territory.

Chapter 14

Inaccessible Heart

"*T*wo things stole the smile from Joseph's face and replaced it with a grim countenance as he approached the Caprock stop. One was the dread of seeing Amy again. The other was his bitter disappointment over his sought-after land. He tightened the reins too sharply and came to a thundering halt, grateful that he had no passengers tossing about in the carriage.

Mrs. Browning and Amy greeted him eagerly —too eagerly.

He gave them a preoccupied hello, going directly to his room. "He'll come out for supper," Mrs. Browning assured the crestfallen Amy. "The wheels of fate turn slowly."

"I don't believe they're turning at all." Amy's eyes glistened with unshed tears, her dreams awash. "I think those wheels of fate have a broken axle!"

Supper brought no hint of Cupid or his arrow for Amy. Joseph kept his eyes carefully averted while seated across the table from her. *What a night for the inn to be empty of guests!* he thought bitterly. *And I the center of attention.*

"What did you find out about your land, Joseph?" Mr. Browning inquired. The inquiry was solicitous rather than probing.

"I've hit a blank wall," Joseph answered, his disappointment bleeding through his reserve. "They sent the papers to Charles to sign just before he left the land. As far as the government is concerned, he still has those papers. It's illegal to duplicate them."

"But in the event Charles is dead?"

"The government would have to have a certificate of death and, of course, that would be impossible for me to obtain. The law requires a document signed by two living witnesses that knew the time and place of his death before they will draw up more papers."

"But after a certain time. . . ?"

"Without those papers, I'd never be able to get a clear deed. The red tape would be endless. I understand that they did it to protect the landholders. It's ironclad."

"Couldn't you still file occupancy claim until. . .until something is settled?"

"Building on land with no title is too risky for me. It's a lovely piece of property, and I'm afraid I had set my heart on it too much. The government would have first priority. They might eventually decide to make it into a military outpost, a national park, anything—whatever their whim. My life's efforts would be lost. I wouldn't have a leg to stand on. No proof of ownership. Mere occupan-

124

cy. I want more than that."

"I can see your point, Joseph. And I'm afraid I'm almost as disappointed as you are."

"How were my children, Joseph?" asked Mrs. Browning.

Joseph cleared his throat, embarrassed. "I'm sorry, Mrs. Browning, I forgot to give you your letter." He pulled Charlotte's wrinkled note from his pocket, reprimanding himself for his carelessness. "And I'm afraid I didn't take very good care of it at that." Then, in answer to her question, "They're fine—and *very* happy."

"I knew they'd be happy."

Amy sought an opportunity to talk to Joseph about the vacant teaching position at Brazos Point. Grace Browning sensed that, but she also discerned that Amy lacked the courage to broach the subject since the young man would not look her direction. So Mrs. Browning took it upon herself to help out in the matter when she had finished reading Charlotte's note.

"Amy has something she needs to discuss with you, Joseph," she opened the way for Amy.

Joseph raised his eyes with a start, something akin to fright showing in their depths. "I. . .I. . .got Jonathan. . .on the train with no problems," he supplied quickly.

Amy gave a shy laugh. "I'm not worried about Jonathan Browning. He's old enough and big enough to take care of himself. I wanted to talk about the opening for a school teacher that you mentioned." Amy steadied her voice with some difficulty.

"Yes?"

"I know someone who would like the position."
Joseph would have seen her dimples had he looked at her.

"Yes, and a real good teacher she'll be for Effie," interjected Grace Browning.

"Now, that's good news! My folks will be glad to hear that!" Joseph unthawed a bit. "Where could I contact this . . .this good teacher?"

Amy's lilting laughter rippled across the table, striking Joseph's ears—and heart. "It's me," she said, not bothering with proper grammar. "I want the position!"

"You?"

"Is there an age limit. . .or specifications. . . ?"

"No, but. . . ."

"Then please may I apply for the job?"

"But what about. . .Jonathan?"

"I discussed it with him the night before he left and he's perfectly agreeable. I'm of age, he says, and it's my decision. I. . .prayed about it, too." Her eyes were misty. "I thought I could fill the vacancy at least temporarily while the school board is looking for a permanent replacement."

"I. . .I don't know about the wages. They're rather low, I'm afraid."

"The wages aren't important. If I need money, I'll contact Jonathan and he'll send me some."

"You. . .I'm sure the school would be fortunate to get you." Still he avoided the expressive violet eyes.

"Would you. . .could you notify them that I'm available? Or tell me who to contact?"

"You're quite sure this is what you should do? It's a very small school, and you might have to room with the parson. . .or maybe Miss Vivian, the former teacher. We

126

haven't a teacher's cabin yet. Miss Vivian was local and had her own home. Besides, that part of the country has been terribly hard hit by a drought this summer. You. . .it probably won't be anything like you are accustomed to."

"Oh, don't worry about me. I'm sure of my decision. I've done some substitute teaching back in Kentucky. I have my certificate."

"I don't doubt your qualifications." Joseph looked down at his gnarled hands. "I. . .well, maybe it's the wisdom of your decision that I doubt!"

She gave another soft laugh. "Mr. Harris, it's something I want to do very much. What do you think my chances are of obtaining the position?"

"I can send an express to Parson Stevens. He's sort of the overseer, the acting head of the school board. I think they'll take you on my recommendation alone. Will you be traveling. . .by train?"

"I could ride the coach as far as Amarillo, then take the train on from there. Where is the closest depot?"

"They've recently put a rail through to The Springs, twelve miles from Brazos Point. Pastor Stevens or my brother Matthew could meet you there."

"This. . .sister of yours that needs special help. . . could you give me any idea what help she might need? To be honest with you, that's the challenge that takes me to the country school."

Amy is employing every tactic, Grace Browning mused, *and doing a mighty good job of forcing Joseph to talk to her! The poor boy is heartblind if he can't see her motives.*

"She's as smart as a whip!" Joseph dropped his self-consciousness when the subject swung to Effie. "She can read anything, but her physical condition keeps her from writing legibly. I fear that her attempts to write on a sheet of tablet would remind you of a mouse falling into the ink-well and skittering about the page with wet feet!"

Amy smiled, enjoying the simile. "Has she ever attended school?"

"Not public school," Joseph chuckled. "But my sister Dessie and I weren't bad teachers for amateurs. She can do math in her head faster than William can work a problem on the chalkboard. Her tests would probably have to be given orally, after hours."

"Can she talk at all, Mr. Harris?"

"Given time, yes. She stumbles over her words—stutters. But I've never seen anybody with *eyes* that talk like Effie's." Joseph stopped, apparently flustered, then hurried on. "It would take a lot of extra time to teach her, I'm afraid."

Why had Joseph hesitated at the mention of eyes? Was it possible that he suddenly remembered the first time our eyes met at the Amarillo stop? Amy rebounded. "Oh, I wouldn't mind the extra time! I suppose that I would have all the time in the world. Until Jonathan returns."

At the name Jonathan, Joseph stirred uneasily in his chair. "I had hoped we could find a teacher that would take Effie."

"You've found one. . .if they'll take me."

"I have no doubts."

"Has. . .Effie always had these problems?"

"Yes, she was born a. . .I believe they call it spastic. She's pretty crippled up in her body—Jim and I call her a 'bent winged angel'—but I've never seen a sharper mind or a sweeter spirit." Amy was easy to talk to and understanding.

"I just can't wait to meet her and help that intelligent mind develop!"

If Joseph will only look at Amy, Grace Browning worried, *surely he can't escape her charms.*

"Are there any discipline problems in the school?" Amy wanted to keep him conversing. "I mean, like older boys? Bullies?"

"No, ma'am. There never has been before."

"How many pupils could I expect to teach?"

"Let's see, there're six from our family, counting Effie. Chester, Alan, Arthur, William and Dessie. There're five Gibsons. That makes eleven. This will be Pauline Steven's last year. That's the parson's daughter. That makes twelve. Miss Myrt's two grandchildren make fourteen. . .and four from the Kopperl community. You'll have around twenty, give or take a couple."

"Just perfect! I'll be too excited to sleep!"

"I'll send a wire tomorrow. If I may be excused, Mrs. Browning?" Joseph pushed back his chair, anticipating escape to his quarters. "I'm. . .I'm not too excited to sleep." He grinned and Amy caught her breath at his handsome ruggedness.

"Have a good night, Joseph," Mrs. Browning called cheerily. "We'll see you on the morrow."

Joseph closed the door to his room, grateful for solitude. *Jonathan Browning, why couldn't you have taken your wife with you and spared me this anguish? And now she is taking herself to my home territory!*

"I'll never break down his wall of resistance!" Amy talked to Grace Browning in a stage whisper. "There may be a vacancy in his heart, but he's got the door nailed

129

shut—and a no trespassing sign posted in plain sight!"

"Never say never!" admonished Grace Browning.

Where have I heard that before? Amy puzzled.

Chapter 15

The Teacher

"We have located a temporary teacher for our school," Pastor Stevens told the church board that doubled as the school board. The six rugged farmers sat solemnly in front of him on the church pews, in their clean overalls and denim shirts. "Her name is Mrs. Jonathan Browning and she has been highly recommended by Joseph Harris. You are to understand that this is only a temporary assignment until we can locate a permanent replacement for Miss Vivian. With this arrangement, school can start on schedule the first of September. That's our goal. All in favor, please say aye."

"Aye."

"Meeting adjourned."

Henry hurried home. "What was th' meetin' all about, Henry?" Martha pried.

"Dessie comes by her inquisitiveness honest," Henry

said dryly.

"Better halves have a right to ask questions, Henry."

"Brother Stevens got an express from Joseph."

"Our Joseph?"

"Who else? He's found us a teacher fer th' school. She's just temporary until we can find a permanent one, but she'll be here in time to start classes on time next month. We voted on her, an' th' whole board voted aye."

"A blessin'!" Martha rejoiced at the good news. "I wonder will she take Effie?"

"I don't know, Martha. Remember, she's just substitutin' till we can get a steady teacher. I wouldn't get my hopes up if'n I was you. But, then again, Joseph knew we was hopin' to get someone who'd teach our Effie."

The community buzzed with excitement at the announcement of the new teacher. However, when word reached Jake Grimes, he protested angrily that he was not invited to the school board meeting. "I'm as much a part of this community as anybody else!" he shouted. "I got kids, too. Just because I ain't a church goin' man is no cause to be cut out of th' votin'. Any place run by a *church* is not democratic!"

"Will he cause a ruckus, Henry?" worried Martha.

"He won't do nuthin' but blubber, Martha. If'n he'd been there, he'da voted no fer th' reason that ever'body else voted aye. Never seen anybody more contrariwise."

Matthew and Pauline offered to drive into The Springs in Pastor Stevens's gig to meet Amy at the train station, relishing the opportunity to be together again before Matthew's departure for college. The plant life along the scenic route, usually eye-pleasing, drooped under a coat of fine, limy dust. The weed-infested fields discouarged any beauty that tried to thrive there. But Matthew and Pauline gave scant heed to any of this. Their days together were numbered. Time was too precious to waste on wilted landscapes.

"I'll miss you, Pauline," Matthew held her hand tightly. "Maybe you'll find somebody else while I'm away."

"Why, Matthew Harris," she scolded gently. "There never was anybody else for me. . .and never will be." Pools of tears stood ready to spill from her loyal eyes.

"I'll come home every chance I get," Matthew promised quickly, touched by her tears.

"And I'll be waiting," she said. "God is my witness." A comforting silence followed, the blissfulness of togetherness sufficient. These two needed no idle chatter as a crutch for their relationship.

Assisted by the conductor, Amy stepped off the train, carrying her trunk and traveling case. Her eyes scanned the crowd that milled about the depot, welcoming and waving. She spotted Matthew without hesitation. "You're Joseph's brother!" she cried, extending her small hand. "And this is. . . ?"

"Pastor Stevens's daughter, Pauline."

"I'm pleased to meet you, Pauline. Joseph told me you would be graduating this year."

"I hope." Pauline smiled demurely.

Amy's blue crepe dress and fashionable hat made her a queenly spectacle in the town and Pauline sat tall, proud to help escort such a beautiful lady. *How did Joseph manage to get a teacher of this quality for the poor, rural school of Brazos Point? And to think that this pretty teacher will be sharing our home! Of course, it is only temporary. That is the bad part.*

133

Whispers circulated about Amy. "She's strikingly beautiful," Matthew told the Harris family that night. "And a lady of etiquette."

"What does that mean, Matthew?" Martha asked.

"Manners," he said without a hint of superiority or shame at his mother's ignorance.

The Harris students listened eagerly to Matthew's account of the new teacher, the throbbing ache of losing their beloved Miss Vivian easing away. "Maybe she can teach th' Grimes kids some manners," William said hopefully. "They sure need some."

"I just hope they don't make trouble for her." Matthew shook his head. "She's too nice to be taken advantage of by uncouth heathens like the Grimes!"

"Matthew!" gasped Martha.

"I'm sorry, Mother," apologized Matthew. "And here I am—the one trying to convert heathens! The Bible does speak about reprobates, though, and I'm not sure but what we have one on our hands in the form of Mr. Grimes."

" 'Taint our'n to judge, Matthew."

Jake Grimes probably regretted being an atheist Sunday when the community met the new teacher at church. "Wouldn't be surprised if'n he was hid in a tree so's not to miss anything," Henry said of the neighbor.

Amy lost no time in stealing the hearts of both young and old. It was agreed that first Sunday that the school was indeed fortunate to have her.

"Brother and Sister Harris, this is Mrs. Jonathan Browning," Pastor Stevens made the introduction along with a slight bow.

"Excuse me, Reverend. It's *Miss* Amy Browning," she blushed prettily.

"Er. . .I. . .my apologies," the pastor stammered awkwardly. "There's been a mistake."

Amy's sense of humor salvaged the day for her and the pastor when she dismissed the error with a wave of her hand. "Jonathan Browning is my brother—that way I don't have to cherish and obey him."

At the dismissal of service, Amy made her way to Effie, who sat patiently on the bench while the rest of the family socialized. Amy had spotted her early in the service and now she knelt beside the seat and took Effie's stiff, bony hand in her own soft grasp. Effie smelled Amy's perfume, recognized the gentleness in her sweet dark eyes, and smiled her most pleasant crooked smile.

"You must be Effie."

"Y-yes."

"I'm Amy Browning, Effie, and I've come to be the school teacher here. . .at least for a little while. Joseph tells me that you would like to enroll in classes this fall. Is that right?"

"Oh, y-yes! M-may I?"

"Of course you may! I'm looking forward to having you in my class. I'd be disappointed if you changed your mind. We'll have a good time studying together, won't we?"

"Y-yes!"

Joseph was right when he said her eyes talked. They spoke volumes. "Joseph said that you could do arithmetic faster in your head than your brother could do figures on the chalkboard."

"J-Joseph is s-sweet."

"He sure is!" Amy dimpled.

"Y-you-ve m-met h-him?"

135

"With pleasure. Do you have any questions?"

"What g-grade will I-I be in?"

"We'll give you a little test and find out. I suspect you'll be right up there with your age group."

"I-I'm slow."

"Don't worry about that, Effie. You and I can have some little meetings after classes and catch up."

"O-okay."

"Any other questions?"

"W-where did you l-live?"

"My home is way back east in Kentucky. I met Joseph on the stagecoach. My brother and I had started to California, but I decided to come here instead. This is more interesting."

"I-I'm glad! Y-you w-will s-stay?"

"I'll stay as long as I'm needed, Effie." She gave Effie's frail hand a gentle pat. "I love it here already."

"Y-you l-look l-like my m-mother."

Amy glanced at Martha, finding no resemblance between herself and the large-framed Harris woman, but supposing this to be Effie's ultimate expression of approval she said graciously, "Why, thank you, Effie. That's nice of you to say a thing like that."

"Y-your e-eyes." Amy looked again at Martha, puzzled. What connection the child found between her eyes and Martha's was a mystery to her.

Conversation at the Harris dinner table that Sunday centered around the newcomer. "She's jest about th' nicest young lady I've ever seen," Martha commented.

"She is at that, Martha," agreed Henry.

"Wonder why Joseph didn't choose her fer his sweetheart?"

"That's his business."

"But Henry, sometimes Joseph worries me. He's gonna fool 'round an' let all th' good 'uns get away while he's dallyin' 'round on that stagecoach!"

"Now, Martha, let's not get into no matchmakin'," Henry remonstrated. "When Joseph gets ready fer a wife, he's twenty-one an' weighs more'n ninety pounds. He's man enough to pick 'is own."

"Jest hope he's *smart* enough," retorted Martha. "He *did* meet this lady, didn't he?"

"I 'spose he'da had to. He's th' one that sent her to us. How else would he 'a knowed 'bout her?"

"Coulda heard 'bout her through somebody else."

"In that case, he'll meet 'er when he next comes home."

"S-she's m-met J-Joseph!" Effie supplied. "On th-the s-stagecoach. H-he t-told her a-about me. A-and she'll t-take m-me in s-school!" Effie's eyes danced.

"She said she would?" Henry asked. "Really?"

"Y-yes. S-she s-said so th-this m-morning."

"Let's pray we can keep 'er awhile, then!"

"Yeah. 'Cause I like her dimples an' I think she's *beautiful*," William said.

"Wish I had dimples," Dessie complained.

"You had 'um when you was a baby, but you went an' outgrew 'em. We have to accept th' way God made us," Martha admonished.

"Some people were just made by a special pattern, I'm thinkin'," Henry interjected.

"S-she l-looks l-like my m-mother."

"She does look like th' picture of Aunt Rebecca, Mama," Dessie substantiated. "Go get th' tintype, Effie, an' let's see.''

Effie stumbled away and returned with Rebecca's photograph, passing it from hand to hand around the table. "Does favor, doesn't she, Mama?" William agreed.

Martha studied the portrait, drawing her forehead into lines of heavy concentration. "Yes, Miss Amy does bear a 'semblance o' Rebecca. 'Specially her eyes.''

Chapter 16

An Unsuccessful Trip

*R*ugged persistence led Jonathan to the Andrews log cabin in Oregon. Bent on his mission, he missed much of the picturesque display of nature about him. Amy would be bereft of the description of the pools of water so crystal clear that the rocks on the bottom ten feet below appeared to be only inches from the surface. Jonathan permitted himself no time for exploring or sightseeing. He pressed on doggedly.

Almost by accident, he stumbled onto the overgrown trail that led to the door where bloodshot eyes set in a blotched face answered his sturdy knock. Mr. Sawyer's word portrait of Carl Andrews proved to be amusingly correct.

"Mr. Andrews? I'm Jonathan Browning."

"Now if you're here for a handout or to collect any bills, you can get off my property!" the intemperate man barked. "Just because I had gold once in my life is no sign I've still got some to hand out."

Jonathan was determined not to be deterred. "Mr. Andrews, I need some information. Perhaps you can help me. May I come in?"

Carl Andrews hesitated, vacillating between slamming the door in Jonathan's face and stepping aside to let him enter. "How'd you find out where I live?"

"Mr. Sawyer in California told me you lived in this area. It has taken me two weeks to find you."

"Old Sawyer!" Mr. Andrews gave a harsh crackling laugh. "Old Sawyer, *I said!*" He opened the door, and Jonathan pushed his way through. "You mean old Sawyer's still kickin'?"

"Oh, yes. He's quite hale and hardy."

"And still chasing the widder that runs the joint where he lives?"

"I wouldn't know about that, Mr. Andrews."

"And still holding on tightfisted to his dough?"

"He's. . .I know nothing of his personal affairs."

"You haven't stated your business, barging in on a self-respecting man like me."

"I'm looking for a relative. . . ." Jonathan stopped in mid-sentence when Carl's rotund wife entered the room. Her round face showed frightened surprise at his presence. There could be no connection between this coarse-featured woman with bright red hair and green eyes and the portrait of the young lady he carried in his valise—not by the wildest stretch of the imagination. *Could this be Carl Andrews's second wife, perhaps? Had Ann died or. . . ?"*

"We don't have no relatives," Carl said flatly. "None

at all."

"I'm looking for an aunt named Ann who married a man by the name of Andrews." Jonathan ignored Carl's lack of cooperation. He knew these kind seldom told the truth.

"Couldn't be my wife. Her name's Melissa."

"I thought you might have some information concerning Aunt Ann."

"Well, I don't."

"She was from Kentucky."

"We never been to Kentucky in our life. Never had no plans of going there. Don't know nobody there. Ain't got no kin there."

"I'm terribly sorry, Mr. Andrews. For you, that is. Because this Ann is heir to a large estate."

"How's that? She is, eh? Well, now, my wife's middle name is Ann. Yep. Melissa *Ann*. Bound to be the gal you're looking for." Carl reversed his story with head-spinning alacrity, winking wickedly at his wife. "You have relatives all over Kentucky, don't you, Ann?" Jonathan had known the magic words would work.

"That's right. Grandma and grandpa, aunts and uncles, brothers and sisters, nieces and nephews, cousins. Why, I'm kin to most everybody in the whole state of Kentucky even if I never lived there myself."

"Is this your first and only wife, Mr. Andrews?"

Carl missed his cue. "Why, certainly. Death ain't parted us yet, and I promised to honor and obey her till death sets me free," he leered. "A lot of times I wished. . . ."

"You got it all back'erds, Carl. It's me that's got to honor and obey and you've got to cherish and furnish.

141

'Twas me what came out on the short end of the handle. Now I should've married Marvin Tucker like my mother wanted me to.''

"Aw, shut up, Melissa. . .I mean, Ann." He lurched at her and she dodged, moving with amazing speed for her bulk. "You're always exputing my word and trying to pick a fight with me! Now let's find out from this good man where to get this here money you've inherited back in good ole Kentucky. And if you mention that prude, Marvin Tucker, one more time. . .I'll. . .I'll. . .I'll find him and smash his skull."

"I'm afraid. . . ."

"Now tell us which relative it is that left us in his will," insisted the inebriated Carl. "We could use that money all right."

"We sure could. You drank up all the pay dirt money."

Carl shot her a murderous look. "Quiet!"

"Have you any children?" asked Jonathan, sure that he was on a cold trail.

"One. A no-good boy. He's sixteen years old and not worth shooting. But don't worry, mister. We'll see that he don't squander this here Kentucky money."

"Ann," Jonathan addressed the imposter, catching her offguard, "what was your maiden name?"

Carl was clever, even loaded with intoxicant. "Browning, of course," he supplied while she hesitated. It surprised Jonathan that he remembered his name.

"I'm sorry, Mr. Andrews," Jonathan kept his face serious in spite of his amusement. "The inheritance isn't on the Browning side of the family."

"Oh, what *was* your maiden name, Melissa. . .uh,

142

Ann?'' Carl sputtered.

"I ain't telling. I'm in line for any wealth in Kentucky.''

Jonathan reached into the traveling case and produced the picture. "Have you ever seen this lady, Mr. Andrews?''

A blank expression betrayed him.

"I've met her!'' Melissa exclaimed, snatching at the snapshot. "Why, I should say so! That's my own sister?''

"Couldn't be,'' Jonathan contradicted. "This lady only had one sister and that was my own mother.'' He looked squarely at Carl's obese wife. "And I don't believe you're my mother.''

Jonathan left disappointed, with Carl shouting curses after him. He had followed a false lead and lost a month on this unfruitful expedition. But this was part of the game. He would simply go back to the drawing board and start over.

His intuition led him back to California. Here he wrote Amy a long and informative letter, posting it to the Caprock Station and asking that the Brownings forward it on to Amy in the event she was elsewhere. He had a strong suspicion that she was in Texas.

Dear Sister

What a time I'm having trying to find Aunt Ann! Whew! Combine a tipsy man and his fleshy wife, neither of whom can tell the truth, and you have quite a pair! An oldtimer in Los Angeles sent me on this fruitless mission to check out the whereabouts of one Carl Andrews in Oregon. I am leaving no stones unturned, regardless of what I find

143

under them!

The trip to Oregon was disappointing. I scarcely took time to see the beautiful country. Strictly business. Admittedly, I was quite relieved to find that the people in Oregon named Andrews were no relation to us, though they tried every way possible to claim kin when they learned there was an inheritance at stake. Why, the old prevaricator tried to convince me she was my own mother! Hogwash!

I'm back in California and will soon take a look at the San Francisco area. You would enjoy California and I'm somewhat lonesome for you. The beach and ocean are incredibly beautiful. Much different from the East Coast. The scenery and climate are fabulous.

Had I known that I would have the good fortune of headquartering at Mrs. Bimski's boarding house, I would have insisted that you come along. You and Mrs. Bimski would make quite a pair! And you never tasted such good breakfast rolls! If you want to join me here, I'll send you a train ticket. You wouldn't, however, be able to follow me on many of my expeditions. My mission takes me into places unfit (and unsafe) for a lady. I'm taking to the miners' shanties next week.

I have made a remarkable discovery since being here in Los Angeles! Remember the uncle that our coach driver, Joseph Harris, asked me to inquire after? I found his name on an old register of the hotel here. This happened to be his former residence. The proprietor remembered him well. I'm sorry to say that he is deceased. I have obtained

144

all the information I could about his death and I visited his grave. Tell Joseph I will share these details with him when I return.

Mrs. Bimski gave me some papers for Joseph. She has held them all these years, waiting for someone to claim them. One of the documents, she said, was Mr. Harris's marriage license. The other is a legal paper concerning some land Mr. Harris had staked claim on in the Territory of New Mexico. I'm sending these papers to you so that you may give them to Joseph. My suspicion is that you would enjoy the personal encounter. Whatever end of his stage line you are on, you'll see him sooner or later.

I have placed a notice in the newspapers everywhere advertising for Aunt Ann as our lawyer suggested. One woman named Minnie Ann Andrews answered the advertisement in Monterey, having some distant connections back East. She proved to be seventy years old and readily agreed that she was no heir to the estate. I found her to be a fascinating old soul, however, who could bake a cherry pie fit for the Governor. She knew of no Andrews in the area that fit the description of Ann. My search would be easier if we had a clearer memory of her husband. I do have hopes that someone will recognize Ann's picture in connection with the Andrews name.

Dear heart, I am by no means giving up! I find the hunt a greater challenge each day and am meeting many interesting people, as well as learning California history. The oldtimer sees to my local education. I am also keeping a day-by-day *diary and will share the details of this journal with you when we are together again.*

Write me at Mrs. Bimski's, my California headquarters. She'll hold my mail for me in safekeeping. And let me know if you want a ticket to the Wild West. I'll see that you are taken care of and have a good time here.

And remember, Sis, never say never!

> *I remain, your loving brother,*
> *Jonathan*

The letter followed Amy to Texas along with the papers. She read the letter twice, digesting every word. As for her uprooting and going to her brother in California, that was out of the question. She told herself that she couldn't disappoint Effie. *But was that the real reason?*

Jonathan mentioned papers on some land. *Can these be the documents Joseph needs to obtain his land? Should I take the papers to Joseph's family? No,* she told herself, *I'd rather give them to him myself.*

So with a quick beat of her heart, she stowed the documents away carefully among her own personal belongings and awaited Joseph's return. . . with eager anticipation.

Chapter 17

Problems at School. . . and Elsewhere

"Teacher, Claude Grimes is out behind th' boys' outhouse smokin'," one of the younger boys reported to Amy. One week into the new school term and trouble had begun. Amy called Claude in to talk to him.

"Besides being against the rules of this school, one careless spark could set the whole brittle countryside on fire," Amy explained to the insolent young man. "If you are caught smoking on the school grounds again, you will be expelled."

"You're just lookin' for an excuse to get shed of me!" flung Claude defensively. "Oh, don't think I don't know your motive. I've met with these kind of tricks before."

"Claude, you are being disrespectful."

"Well, I ain't aimin' to take no guff off a woman teacher!" Claude Grimes stalked out of the schoolhouse and went home.

"Why you home at midday?" Mrs. Grimes asked, but Claude strode through the barn dwelling sullenly, looking for Jake. He found his father in the cedar brakes, partaking of his hidden brew.

"What's th' problem this time?" Jake questioned belligerently. "School?" He slid his crock jug back into its thistle nest.

"Teacher ain't playin' fair."

"What! Already? We might as well get things straightened out an' settled up from th' start. This is a free country with free education for all an' we have our constitutional rights. You sure you warn't at blame, Claude?"

"I'm never at blame, Paw. Teachers pick on me because I'm behind on my studies and I'm bigger'n all the rest. 'Specially wimmen teachers. I hate wimmen teachers! This one has already started giving me trouble. I think I'll just quit."

"You won't do nary a thing, Claudie. I'm determined you're to get your education. Now tell me about th' problem an' I'll straighten it out with th' school board. No need messin' with some good-fer-nuthin' teacher."

"Well, someone told a big fat lie on me an' she belittled me in front of th' whole class. Even threatened to expel me, so I up an' walked out. I shore ain't givin' her th' pleasure of kickin' me out! I says to myself, 'Paw wouldn't want me puttin' up with this treatment.' An' you wouldn't, would you?"

"Course not. What was th' lie about?"

"Uh. . .some of th' little kids said I was tryin' to set th' school on fire. A'purpose. Now why would I want to do that?"

148

"You hadn't ort to pay no attention to little kids, Claude."

"I wouldnt've, but teacher made somethin' big out'n it."

"First time you ever been accused of arsony. I don't like that a tall."

"An' besides, th' teacher—Miss Amy—shows partiality, like everywhere else we been. She has this *pet* pupil that looks like a scarecrow an' stutters. She can't even write her name on th' chalkboard. She's retarded. Teacher spends hours with th' kid, neglectin' th' rest of th' classes."

"What's a kid like that doin' in school nohow?"

"You got me there, Paw. Teacher has to give her all sorts of special attention. Me an' Sonny don't ever get no attention."

"Does she mistreat Sonny?"

"Yessiree. Just today she told Sonny to sit down and get quiet. She warn't doin' nuthin' but borrowin' some chalk from a boy. An' she made Sonny tell her real name out loud, an' she calls her Sandra instead of Sonny. She said Sonny warn't no name for a lady."

"You're not spoofin' me, Claudie?"

"Nosiree. Ask Sonny if you don't believe me!"

When Sonny came home from school, Jake accosted her. "Sonny, is it a fact that your teacher is favorin' some students in th' class above the others?"

"Tell 'im like it is, Sonny. Tell Paw she favors all th' Harris brats, but 'specially one," warned Claude, narrowing his eyes threateningly.

"Well, there's this little crippled girl. . . ."

"See, I told you, Paw."

149

"What's 'er name?" demanded Jake with a hiccough.

"Effie Harris."

"I'll go see the preacher tomorrow. He's head of th' school board. An' if we can't get no satisfaction here we'll go to higher government powers. . .all th' way to Washington, D. C., if necessary. I mean to get results!"

"An' what do you expect me to do? Sit an' be humiliated by a woman teacher?"

"You stand right up for your rights, Claudie. An' if I hear tell of you turnin' yeller about it, I'll handle *you*. I ain't raisin' no coward. An' get this clear in your head— ain't no teacher going to expel one of th' *Grimes* kids! They got as much right to a desk in th' schoolroom as th' rich kids or th' teacher's pets!"

Jake staggered over to the parsonage the next day, nettled and ready for battle. "I got a matter to take before th' school board," he announced airily to Pastor Stevens. "I hear you're th' head of th' committee."

"Yes, sir. Acting chairman." Pastor Stevens motioned Jake toward a chair, but he disdained to sit, pacing like an angry animal.

"It's a problem that concerns th' new schoolteacher."

Brother Stevens drew his brows together to resemble two black caterpillars facing each other. The smoking incident had already reached his ears and he was highly displeased. "Complaint?"

"You can call it that if you want to. Hit's about my kids. They're bein' picked on 'cause they're behind in their learnin'. Th' teacher has done threatened to expel my Claudie an' school ain't been goin' but a week. Ain't no teacher going to expel one of my kids, Mister. D'ya hear? This is a free country an' they have as much right to books as your kids or anybody else's."

"Ahem," Pastor Stevens interrupted. "Mr. Grimes, I understand that your son was caught behind the school's. . .er, property, smoking a cigarette. That is against school rules and is grounds for dismissal. The teacher was very lenient not to dismiss your son at once."

"Lies! Lies!" shouted Jake, beside himself with rage. "See what I told you! Some of th' kids that don't like Claude told th' fine teacher that lie, didn't they? Tattletalers. Did she see him smokin' herself? I thought not. An' it can't be proved, can it?"

"Why, Mr. Grimes. . . ."

"This happens everywhere we go. Someone tells a lie on one of my children an' gets 'um in trouble with th' teacher. Then th' teacher believes th' lies an' takes a dislikin' to my children. 'Tain't fair. I demand an apology from th' teacher fer shamin' my Claudie in front of th' whole class."

"We feel, Mr. Grimes, that Miss Amy is very fair and. . . ."

"No, she ain't one bit fair! Fact is, Mister Parson, she has *pets* in th' class. She plays favorites. Favoritism I hate. Some girl named Effie gets special attention while th' rest of th' classes go abeggin' for teachin'."

"Effie's a cripple and requires more. . . ."

"Yeah, that's what Claudie said. I'm pleased to hear you admit'n to it. Ain't no cripple girl got no business nor rights in a regular school. Claudie says she stutters an' can't even write her name on th' chalkboard. They need to put her in an asylum where she b'longs. All she's doin' is takin' up th' teacher's time what should be spent with smart kids like Claudie an' Sonny."

"Mr. Grimes, I beg your pardon, but Effie is extremely intelligent. . . ."

"If I can't get no satisfaction out of you, Mr. Stevens,
I'll appeal to th' State Board of Education to have th' girl
removed from school so that th' other pupils can get th'
teacher's rightful attention. Don't like to go over your
head in nuthin', but my kids are goin' to have fair schoolin'
or I'll know why. Th' government ain't payin' th' teacher
to spend her time on simpletons. I've won before. . .and
I'll win again!" He stumbled off, muttering oaths.

"How'd you come out with th' conference, Paw,"
Claude asked, home from a stormy classroom day that
left Amy near tears.

"They ain't gonna do nuthin' to uphold our side of
this argument, Claudie," spat Jake. "Just like ever'where
else."

"Don't worry, Paw. I'll handle it myself. I have a good
idea."

"What's that, Claudie?"

"I'll make school so miserable for that little teacher's
pet that she'll be glad to stay home from school from now
on. An' it won't be hard because she's so spoiled an' used
to gettin' her own way. Then when she's out of th' way,
some of th' rest of us can have some education, too."

"Sounds like a good idea, Claudie. Just don't be too
obvious about it. Teacher'll stand agin' you if you make
any slips."

"I won't make no slips, Paw."

"Do you think gettin' rid of that one rotten kid will
stop th' trouble?"

"It'll make a big difference, Paw. If it don't, we'll do
something else."

152

The Harris family hashed over the school disturbances at the supper table. "It was Alan that told on Claude for smoking, Mama," Dessie said. "An' Claude talked spiteful to Miss Amy when she cornered him. I'm plumb scared of that boy!"

"M-me, too," Effie paled. "H-he d-don't l-like me!"

"I feel sorry for Miss Amy," William said. "She's tryin' hard to be nice to Claude an' Sonny. I wish I was big enough to wallop Claude Grimes."

"An' Sonny sits back an' swears at Miss Amy under her breath," Dessie reported. "An' you know what, Mama? She come to school today with her face painted like a Jezebel! She puckered her red, red lips an' whistled at Jesse Gibson. Miss Amy sat her in th' corner, but she winked at Jesse from th' corner. She's. . .she's *wicked!*"

"I hope Miss Amy don't up an' quit," worried Henry.

"I d-do, too," Effie choked on her words. "S-she's th-the b-best t-teacher in th-the w-world."

"William, I made a plate o' chicken fer th' Stevenses an' Miss Amy. We want Miss Amy to feel our support," Martha said. "Soon's you get through eatin', I want you to take it to 'um."

"Yes'm."

"An' don't dally, William," Henry warned. "I want you back afore sundown, with all th' trouble there's been."

The day, nearing completion, obviously planned to leave its sizzling heat behind. Brazos Point had never seen a hotter September. William rolled up his shirtsleeves as high as he could get them, bearing the platter of chicken carefully on his sun-bronzed arms. He spurned the urging of his burning feet to go faster, so as not to chance

153

spilling his precious cargo.

He had almost reached the bridge with the towel-covered dish when Claude stepped out of the scrub oak thicket. "Where you goin'?"

William kept walking, giving Claude no attention, swallowing his fright.

"What you got there?" Claude moved closer.

Still William did not answer. He hastened his steps, fear mounting.

"Cat got your tongue?" Claude closed in on William. "Ummm. I smell fried chicken." He grabbed for the covered dish, but William tightened his grip. Then, in one quick twist, Claude dumped the contents of the platter onto the parched ground. "My dog's been hungry fer some good old fried chicken fer a long time. Thanks. Say thank you, Spotty."

"Bully!" William spat the word and turned to flee with stinging eyes, leaving the undernourished hound to his repast.

"Teacher's pet!" Claude's words were hurled after him.

Chapter 18

The Rescue

"William, where did you stake out Bossie yesterday?" Martha asked at breakfast as she ladled mush into the ironstone bowls, which were brown with age and use.

"Down by th' river where Papa told me, Mama. Ain't no grass no place else. Why?"

"When Henry brought her in fer milkin' last night, she'd already been milked. That's why we're short on milk this mornin'."

"Maybe Bossy's goin' dry."

"No, she ain't goin' dry. She gave plenty of milk till last night. Somebody beat me to th' milkin'."

Nobody asked who. Everybody knew who.

"Wish we'da trained her to kick strangers." This was from William.

"William!"

Martha sparingly saved back a pint jar of milk for Effie's lunch. She stationed herself on the front porch to see her children off to school, a habit she had practiced every day since Joseph's first day in grade school. William pulled Effie on the sled Henry had reconstructed, dust from the powder-filled weeds beside the trail tailing up into a choking cloud.

"Bless my little Effie," Martha murmured. "Never seen 'er so happy. She takes to school as natural as a pig takes to th' mudhole!" She turned back to the house, a prayer on her lips—a prayer for Amy.

The sinister quiet of the morning classes unnerved Amy. The air was charged with impending disaster. Claude sat staring hard at Effie, a smirk on his whiskery face. What mischief was he plotting?

"Sandra, it is your time to recite," Amy reminded.

Sonny ignored Amy. "Sandra. . . ."

"I won't answer to that girl name."

"That's your legal name, Sandra. And you will respond when addressed properly or take a failing grade." Amy was firm.

"I'll take a failing grade."

Amy passed on to the next pupil.

Bedlam broke out at noon when Effie opened her jar of milk. While Amy had her back turned, Claude slipped up behind Effie's desk. "Teacher's pet," he hissed through clenched teeth so that Amy could not hear. "I owe your family a fish." With that, he dropped a dead minnow into Effie's milk.

Effie gave a low cry and Amy turned around in an instant, but Claude wore a pleasant, innocent expression.

"What's wrong, Effie?" Amy asked solicitously.

"M-my m-milk!" The dead shiner floated to the top

of the jar.

"Claude! Did you put the little fish in Effie's milk?"

"I was just going to show it to her an' it slipped out of my hand an' fell into her milk, Miss Amy," he vowed. Then he shuffled to his desk and watched out of the corner of his eye. The best was yet to come.

Effie struggled with the latch on her lunch pail. Amy bend to help her unclasp it. *Oh, boy, this is going to be good! Even better than I thought!* Claude anticipated with glee. He hadn't counted on the teacher's involvement.

The lid of the pail flew open, and out jumped the lizard Claude had imprisoned there. Effie fainted and Amy screamed. Dessie dropped her biscuit in the scramble and it was trampled underfoot.

"Quick!" Amy panted, handing her dainty white handkerchief with the tatted lace trim to William. "Go out to the pump and wet this, William. Hurry!"

Amy bathed Effie's ashen face, feeling for her pulse. She had never been more terrified—nor frustrated. She knew who the culprit was.

When Effie revived with a wan smile of appreciation, Claude sauntered over to Amy. "Is there anything I can do to help, Miss Amy?" he asked, ill-concealed mockery in his voice.

"Yes, you can help by apologizing to Effie!" Amy was furious.

"Apologize? For what?"

"Claude Grimes, you *know* what!"

"I shain't apologize to that scarecrow for anything." Claude pointed an accusing finger at Effie. "T-teacher's l-little p-pet," he mimicked.

This will be my last day of teaching, Amy made up

157

her mind. *If I can't maintain order, I'm finished. Claude Grimes has me bested. With mischief like this, Effie will suffer more harm than good. This linen handkerchief is my white flag of defeat. Claude knows it and I know it. Look at his smug expression! I'll write to Jonathan for a ticket to California. I'll explain to Pastor Stevens tonight.* She bowed her head wearily. The pain in her head was superceded only by the pain in her heart.

In a flash, Claude was collared by someone much stronger than himself. He cowered under the mighty hand. "Yes, you will apologize. And properly!"

Amy looked up into the determined face of Joseph as he marched Claude by his collar to Effie's desk, tightening his grip on the surprised young rebel's neck with each step. "Say you're sorry."

"Turn me loose!"

"I said, say you're sorry."

"I'm sorry."

"Say it like you mean it." Joseph applied more pressure.

"I'm really sorry, Effie."

"Now apologize to your teacher."

"I'm sorry, Miss Amy."

"Do you mean it?"

"Yes, sir!"

"If I ever catch you harassing Effie or the teacher again, young man, your punishment will be such that you'll forever wish you hadn't. Do you understand?"

"Yes, sir."

"Do you *thoroughly* understand?"

"Yes, *sir!*"

Amy arose from her desk to thank Joseph. But he was

gone.

Her knees still shook and her head throbbed as she prepared the assignments for the rest of the day. But Claude Grimes behaved like a prince—though a very scared one—throughout the remaining classes. He was even nice. Amy felt her nerves unwinding. There would be order now with Claude conquered. She did not know, however, that Sonny had slipped out unnoticed to bear the news of the day's fracas to Jake.

A quarter hour before dismissal, Jake stubbed his toe on the threshhold and fell into the schoolhouse, balancing himself by grabbing the nearest desk.

"You!" he confronted Amy. "You teacher! I demand to know what's goin' on in this school!" His beard, saturated with tobacco juice, worked up and down as his anger mounted.

"Your son. . . ."

"Now look here, teacher. Don't be accusin' my son of meanness he never done! You're discriminatin', that's what. I've come to take care of you."

"Mr. Grimes, if you care to discuss this matter civilly. . . ." Amy's bravery was all on the surface. Inside she crumbled. A tremor that felt like an earthquake began in the pit of her stomach.

"I won't have my children bamboozled by no woman teacher! This is a free country an' education's free for all. Now, you're gonna get down on your hands an' knees an' *repent* to my son for humiliatin' him before th' whole class. D'ya hear?" He edged closer to Amy. She instinctively backed away. His hot breath smelled of cheap liquor. The younger children cowered, while the older ones stared open-mouthed. William flung himself between Jake and Amy, only to be slung aside by the bleary-eyed Jake. "Now bow!" he demanded.

He thrust out a dirty hand to grasp Amy's arm when a form, with lightning speed, pinned his arms behind him. Jake tried to twist free, but was unequal to the strength of his captor.

"You'll not touch the teacher, Mister," Joseph said with authority. "This is her classroom and her word goes here. If you don't like her way of running it, take your children and leave!"

"You ain't tellin' me what to do. . ." Jake began, but Claude intervened.

"Paw," he warned, "you'd better not mess with that guy. He must be some kind of law officer. You'll end up in jail."

Joseph held Jake unrelenting. "Would you like to walk out peaceably or be carried out bodily?" he asked. "You can take your choice."

"I'll go! I'll go! Turn me loose!" Jake implored, unsteady with strong drink.

"Oh, no. You won't go without a word of pardon."

"Pardon me, teacher."

"You mean it?"

"I. . .I mean it."

"And if I ever catch you in this classroom again—or even on the school grounds—you'll wish I hadn't," Joseph assured. Then he escorted Jake to the door. "And you'd better never forget it."

Still shaken, Amy signaled William to pull the bell announcing the day's end. Joseph returned for Effie.

"O-oh, J-Joseph!" Effie clung to him. "Y-you're so b-brave!"

The compliment disconcerted Joseph. "I. . .I just never could tolerate anyone mistreating a. . .a lady." *Someone had to protect the wives of men like Jonathan Browning who ignored the Bible admonition to "cleave."*

"Mr. Harris." Color came back to Amy's blanched face. Her dimples appeared magically "Thank you. But. . . how did you happen to know?"

"I was passing down the road on my way home when William signaled me. I knew something was amiss when William waved that white handkerchief and dashed madly into the building. That's when I found the boy insulting you. . .and Effie. This time was just. . .providence. I simply came to school to pick Effie up and carry her home."

"You saved my teaching career, Mr. Harris."

"I owed it to you. If my memory serves me right, I told you there were no bullies."

"They moved here in your absence, I believe."

"I'm glad I could be of service. Violence doesn't come natural with me."

"You did a noble deed."

"Thank you."

"And Mr. Harris. . .I had a letter from Jonathan."

"He is well?"

"Quite well. Aunt Ann is giving him the chase of his life. He hasn't seen the hem of her garment yet, but he sent some important papers for you."

"Important papers? For *me?*"

"Yes, sir. I have them in my room at Pastor Stevens's house. Could you stop by for them?"

"Will after supper be convenient?"

Amy's headache was gone.

Chapter 19

Important Documents

"*O*h, goody! Joseph's home!" The children clamored around, all trying to talk at once.

"Wow! Joseph, you came to school just at th' right time today!" Dessie said admiringly. "Mama, Joseph sure put th' fear o' God in Mr. Grimes."

"Mr. Grimes don't believe there's a God, Dessie," reminded William.

"He believes there's a Joseph Harris, though!" Dessie laughed.

"We got *turrible* neighbors moved in over at th' old Robbins place, Joseph." This came from young Chester.

"You know what Claude done, Joseph?" supplied Alan. "He stole William's big catfish right off'n his trotline."

"An' told me he didn't get nothin' o' mine!" William added. "He said since he's an American an' th' catfish was, too, he had as much right to th' fish as I did."

"H-he p-paid the f-fish b-back today," giggled Effie.

"An' he snatched a plate o' chicken from William that Mama was sendin' to Teacher," was Arthur's contribution.

"Fed it to his dog," William added again.

"And m-milked the c-cow d-dry."

"An' got caught smokin' at school."

"An' Sonny Grimes swears bad words."

"Which boy was Sonny?" Joseph asked.

"Sonny ain't a boy! She's a girl that paints her lips red an' winks an' whistles at all th' boys."

Martha laughed. "Joseph, it's not that I hain't raised my family not to talk disfavorable o' th' neighbors!"

"But it's ever bit true," vouched Henry, chuckling. "An' then some! Brazos Point is goin' to be obliged to elect a sheriff if'n things get much worse!"

"C-Claude th-thought J-Joseph was s-sheriff!"

"What was going on when I came by and you motioned me to the classroom, William?" Joseph questioned. "I just heard the boy shout that he wasn't going to apologize."

"Claude Grimes first put a minnow in Effie's milk. He thought that nobody was watchin', but I seen him do it. He said it was an accident, which it wasn't. He's good at tellin' lies. Then when Effie opened her lunch box, out jumped a lizard an' scared poor Effie so bad she fainted. It scared Teacher, too. Her lips quivered and her hands shook bad. I felt sorry for her. Course nobody could *prove* who put the minnow there or the lizard, but it's pretty obvious."

"C-Claude doesn't l-like me," Effie said.

"But why, Effie?" Joseph teased, "You didn't pinch him, did you?"

"N-no," Effie grinned. "He-he c-calls me t-teacher's pet."

"Well, I don't think he'll give you or your teacher any more trouble. At least I hope not."

"If'n he does, I'm afeared we won't keep our teacher long," sighed Henry.

"An' that would be tragic, fer all th' children love 'er so an' she's doin' Effie a world o' good," Martha added.

When Joseph departed for the parson's house after supper, speculation ran high. "Maybe he's goin' to see Miss Amy, Mama. Wouldn't that be just too nice?" Dessie suggested. "If'n he'd choose Miss Amy fer his sweetheart, I mean."

"Now listen to me, all of you!" They quietened at Martha's command. "Sometimes if'n flowers er left alone, they'll blossom. But pickin' at 'um ruins 'um. I don't want to hear nary one o' you teasin' Joseph 'bout Miss Amy. Don't say nary a word. Do you understand?" Heads nodded. "Joseph's old enough to select his own sweetheart, without our help. Talkin' er hintin' might just turn him away from 'er. An' you wouldn't want that, would you?" Heads shook. "Then mum's th' word." A solemn seal fell on the small lips.

Pastor Stevens let Joseph in with a cordial handshake while Mrs. Stevens insisted that he come into the dining room for a slice of cake.

"I've just had supper, Sister Stevens," Joseph protested.

"Oh, but you can find room for a piece of cake!" she insisted. "It's a butter poundcake. Amy made it from a

Kentucky recipe and it's the best I've ever tasted!" Joseph marveled at the ripening personality of the shy pastor's wife. He remembered when her meek quietness forbade her to utter a whole sentence. Apparently Jonathan's wife, full of sunshine, had transformed a closed bud into an open bloom.

"Anyhow, we want you to visit for a spell. We haven't seen you in weeks," Parson Stevens said.

Joseph took a chair as far removed from Amy as possible. He congratulated himself that the pain of finding her unavailable had grown less cutting, though she was no less lovely.

"Mr. Harris saved my life today, Pastor Stevens," she said, cheeks rosy and eyes twinking. "And I'll be forever grateful."

"How so?"

"Mr. Grimes got loose and came to school!"

"Mr. Grimes. . .came to *school?*" Color drained from Brother Stevens's face.

"Yes, sir."

Brother Stevens turned to Joseph. "Mr. Grimes is a real troublemaker, Joseph. He's been here complaining to me about the extra time Amy gives Effie. He says that Effie shouldn't be allowed to attend public school."

"Sometimes I think Claude and Sandra shouldn't be permitted to attend," Amy laughed. "They're most disruptive and disrespectful."

"Mr. Grimes threatened to take his case to the State Board of Education," the pastor frowned. "On grounds of favoritism."

"I don't think you have to worry about him anymore," Joseph said modestly. "Not after today."

"Mr. Harris handled Mr. Grimes pretty well, Pastor. And in the nick of time, too. To be quite honest, I had decided this was my last day to teach school. I was mentally tendering my resignation!"

"And that would have been a catastrophe for Brazos Point. All the children like the teacher you sent us, Joseph."

"With the exception of two," Amy put in.

"I can't exactly take the credit for sending her, Brother Stevens," admitted Joseph. "She volunteered."

"I've never found anything more rewarding than working with your little sister, Mr. Harris. If the Grimes', the state, or the angels take her away from me, my resignation will be automatic. Have you noticed she is crossing some of her language barriers? She stutters less already."

"Yes, I noticed."

"I hope the terror Claude caused her today doesn't set us back."

"I think she'll get over it," Joseph assured. "She's one tough little gal."

"Our community has never been called upon to cope with anything like this family of Grimes in the past," Brother Stevens said. "I'm sure other communities have. It's been a real. . .trial."

"We need Mr. Harris here all the time to police the place!" Amy laughed. "Claude thinks he's an officer of the law."

"We'll get him a badge if it'll help!"

Joseph found Mrs. Stevens's appraisal of Amy's cake no exaggeration and enjoyed a second piece with little persuasion. Amy noticed with girlish delight.

"Did Mr. Browning say when he would be returning?" Joseph asked Amy, by way of reminding her of his errand here.

"No, sir, but he sent some papers to you that he said were very valuable." She disappeared into her room for the documents.

"I can't imagine what papers Mr. Browning would send to me," Joseph remarked to the pastor with a puzzled look, but Amy was back in mere seconds.

"Here they are." She handed them to Joseph. "Jonathan came across someone who knew your uncle, and they had these legal documents put away in hopes of locating a relative. One is a copy of your uncle's marriage license, Jonathan said. The other concerns some land he staked claim on."

Joseph sat forward in his chair with a start. "The lost papers! On the land in the Territory! Then. . .Uncle Charles is dead?"

"Yes, I'm terribly sorry to bear the unhappy news, Mr. Harris. Jonathan happened to find his name on the registry at the hotel where he signed in, and he obtained a few details from the proprietor. He said he would relay the information to you on his return trip."

"I knew in my heart that Charles was. . .deceased. I did my grieving years ago. These papers mean. . .well, they mean an awful lot to me. They mean I'll have a chance to get my land after all." Joseph's voice was deep with emotion.

"You will be relocating right away, Mr. Harris?" Amy hoped not, and Joseph sensed that.

"I more or less contracted the coach driving job for one year. I told Jim Collins—the husband of your. . .Mr.

Jonathan's cousin, Charlotte, that I'd try to stick with the job for a year." *Am I making sense?* Joseph wondered silently.

Amy pondered. *Jonathan's cousin, Charlotte? Why couldn't Joseph have just said my cousin?*

"The railroads are giving us stiff competition," Joseph continued, "and we'll probably just close the route out next year. That's all the time I'll need, though. By then, I hope to get started ranching."

"We had hoped you'd locate around here," Pastor Stevens said. Then he laughed, "We need a good sheriff!"

"The West calleth," grinned Joseph. "And I'm not sure I'd want to handle people like these troublemakers on a regular basis. One bust is enough."

"Will you see Matthew while you're home?" Pauline had entered the room, looking radiantly in love.

"Yes, I plan to drive in to The Springs and see him before I return. Mother says he hasn't been home since he started to college, but he sent a note that he's doing well and likes it."

"Yes, I've had several notes." Pauline blushed and exited.

"Pauline is moaning the blues." Amy's laugh was light. "She and Matthew do make a fetching couple. . .like Sarah and Hank Gibson. Mr. Harris, you have the most adorable little niece I've ever seen. I can hardly keep my hands off her every Sunday at church."

"Little Sally Rebecca is coming to see me tonight." Joseph grasped the opportunity to conclude his visit politely. "So I'd best be getting back home. Please send my deepest thanks to Mr. Browning for sending these documents and I'm anxious to hear all he has learned

169

about Uncle Charles. Will he be coming here or will you be going?''

"I really don't know his plans, Mr. Harris. You'll probably see him before I do! If he wants to see me, he'll have to come here, because I can't leave my teaching!''

Now isn't that an unusual attitude for a wife to have toward her husband? thought Joseph.

Chapter 20

The Enemy of Death

The viselike dearth pinched every household—every one, that is, except Pastor Stevens's. Amy insisted on paying room and board, an amount that exceeded her earnings, which amply covered their expenses. Besides, Henry Harris had paid an enormous sixty dollars in tithes.

Sarah and Hank showed up at Martha's table frequently, their stock of supplies dwindling. The mortgage Henry had been able to execute kept the wolf of hunger appeased. Martha spent frugally.

Sally Rebecca wasted no time in stealing her grandfather's heart. "She's a Harris dead out!" Henry bragged to Joseph, as he entwined a soft black ringlet about his weather-cracked finger. Little Rebecca patted his face, giving him a slobbery kiss. "An' she loves 'er grandpappy!"

"She's gettin' a new tooth, grandpappy!" Hank

boasted, his fatherly pride exploding. "Her first one."

"When Rebecca comes to th' Harris house, she steals th' whole show, Uncle Joseph," explained Dessie.

"So I see," agreed Joseph. "And I also see why." She dimpled as Amy did when she laughed.

"Joseph, have you heard?" Sarah was excited. "Eunice has a beau! Can you believe it? He's from an upstandin' family, too. He came over from Eulogy to fix Miss Vivian's chimney an' Miss Vivian invited Eunice over to meet him. I think it was love at first sight on his part. 'Course Eunice always kinda favored you."

"Joseph's lettin' all th' good 'uns get away." Martha's words carried an underlying message.

"Eunice'll make a good wife all right," Sarah supported. "She can cook good an' she likes tendin' babies."

Eunice Gibons. What my family says is true. Eunice is a jewel. But would it be fair to take a girl to wife and compare her to Amy Browning until eternity. . .only to have her come up woefully short? He couldn't do Eunice— or any other young lady—like that.

When Joseph went into town to visit Matthew, Sissy Rhodes hailed him down before he could make his escape. He had not thought of her—or any other courting prospect—since he met Amy.

"You're back, Joseph!" Sissy gushed. "For good, I hope?"

"I'm afraid not." Joseph tipped his hat. "I just came for a short visit with Matthew before I return to the coach route." Sissy's charms, which once would have turned his head, now failed to appeal to Joseph at all. She could not hold a light to Amy. *Here I am doing it again. Will I never cease comparing all girls to Mrs. Jonathan Browning?*

"But what luck!" she cried. "I'm having a party this very night. Of course you'll come. We'll turn it into a homecoming bash for our famous coach-driver-come-home. What great fun!"

"I. . .there's something my mother needs and I'll be returning to the country. . . ."

"Oh, that's no problem! We can change the party to tomorrow night. That'll give me ample time to notify the whole gang. We'll invite Matthew and he can bring along his girlfriend, Pauline Stevens. A party in your honor! Mother will be beside herself!"

"Thank you, but I'm afraid I must excuse myself." Sissy's ruse failed. And she thought she had a slip-free noose. Joseph had eluded her again. She could not figure out how she had let that happen.

Joseph bought a sizable supply of staples for Martha and candy for the children. How his family was surviving in spite of the devastating crop failure and deadly drought mystified him. He wondered if his father had money saved back for such emergencies.

Joseph was unloading groceries when he noticed Henry's look of grave concern. He sat rocking Rebecca. She slept fitfully.

"Is our little one sick?" Joseph inquired.

"Been fevery all afternoon. Cuttin' teeth, probably. But I don't like to see a baby sick. Worries me."

"How did you find Matthew?" Martha emptied the box of food thankfully.

"Matthew's different, Mama. I can't quite put my finger on it. He seems so settled and sober, like he's grown up five years since I saw him last. I believe he has something on his mind."

"Matthew takes studyin' serious, Joseph."

When Sarah came for Rebecca, Eunice Gibson was with her. In her faded cotton dress, meticulously starched and pressed with the sadiron, she embodied simplicity and sweetness. *How would she look on the ranch. . .cooking, gardening, sewing?* Joseph wondered. Her glad greeting assured Joseph that it was not too late for him. He had no doubts that she would forsake all to go with him to The Territory. She would be hardy and loyal. But when Eunice smiled up at him expectantly, something went cold in his heart. He escaped out the back door and stood looking miserably into the chicken pen, seeing neither roosters nor hens. He was glad the young man from Eulogy liked her. It let him off the hook with an easy conscience.

The baby's fever had not abated. Her skin was hotter, her face more flushed. "Better watch her careful, Sarah," Martha admonished. "Babies can lose flesh fast. Has she got the run-offs?"

"Real bad, Mama."

Martha ransacked the pantry for the one jar of blackberries she had saved just for this purpose. She boiled the juice down to a thick syrup and spoon-fed it to Rebecca. "Now ever' hour, Sarah," she instructed, "give 'er one tablespoon o' applesauce an' one tablespoon o' buttermilk. That's to replace th' linin' o' her stomach an' intestines she's losin' with th' diarrhea. My mama told me this old wives' formula an' I saved Matthew with it."

"Better stay here tonight, Sarah, an' let me help you sit up with 'er," Henry advised. "I don't much want you takin' 'er out o' my sight." But Sarah said she and Hank would manage between the two of them.

"I'll help 'er if'n she needs," Eunice offered.

174

Before dawn, however, Sarah and Hank brought Rebecca back. "She's gettin' worse, Mama." Sarah's eyes were swollen from crying. "An' I'm shore scared. Even water goes right through 'er now. An' she's gettin' awful weak. Won't even try to hold up her head. Hank's afraid it's distemper-like."

Henry put the baby on his shoulder, her hot body burning his chest. "I think it's time to start prayin'," he said.

"We been prayin' all night, Papa." Sarah wiped her eyes and Hank looked helpless.

"An' I think we'd best get Joseph up an' send him fer Doc Murphy," Martha insisted. "Babies can take real bad fast."

Joseph set Adam at a run. *What would my father do if anything happened to the apple of his eye, "the continuation of myself" as he described the child to me when Rebecca was born? He would take it worse than losing one of his own. His back would stoop a little lower and his hair would grow a little grayer.*

Dr. Murphy goaded his horse as fast as he dared trust the buggy wheels on the rough road. He hurried into the house without knocking, black satchel swinging from his big hand. He had fought off the death angel in this household before. Henry handed him the inert child.

He said nothing for several minutes, but his face was taut. "She's so far gone, it'll be a miracle if she pulls through," he finally told them plainly. Dr. Murphy was not one to evade issues or pad the truth with false hopes. "Children this young can dehydrate amazingly fast."

"I thought she was jest teethin'," Sarah sobbed. "If'n I'd a knowed. . . ."

"Now don't go ablamin' yerself," Martha scolded tenderly.

"That may have started it," Dr. Murphy explained. "Upset stomach. Diarrhea. Then a fever takes over and somewhere the little system reaches the point of no return. We lose a lot of children this way. Especially along about their first summer. I have a tonic, but I don't believe it will help. Prepare yourselves for the worst."

Dr. Murphy worked diligently with the little body, but got no response. Effie heard the doctor's verdict and buried her face in her pillow so the rest of the family would not hear her racking sobs. Why must a lovely baby, all sound and whole, die?

Joseph paced the yard. He had missed the agonies of Robert's death, but this one offered no means of escape. He ached deeply for the whole family. If he should label this year, as was his habit of doing, it would be "the year of losses." He had lost the girl he never had, Papa had lost the crops, and Martha was about to lose her first granddaughter. It seemed there should be some way to balance life's ledger.

Joseph marveled at Martha's fortitude. She got the children up, fed them buttermilk pancakes, and sent them to school. With her hands she said it—life must go on. Only Effie was allowed to remain at home; she had spent her strength crying. For some wounds, there was no comfort.

When Amy received the news of Rebecca's illness from the Harris children, she suffered along with the family. With a heavy heart, she listened mechanically to the recitations and granted a long recess. The classroom held her body, but the Harris home held her heart.

"Life and death come to all of us," Dr. Murphy said.

The city folks said he was part preacher. "And it's not in our power to change that fact. But it does seem a tragedy to lose a baby this beautiful. I hope to see the day when we have great hospitals and deaths like this can be prevented."

"Do you think, doctor, that she could be saved in a hospital?"

"Yes, I do. If the liquid that babies like this lose could be replaced through their veins, they wouldn't have to die."

"Some things only God can fix, Doctor," Martha said quietly. "An' we have to trust His wisdom an' leave th' decision in His hands. 'Tain't easy, but He knows best."

"She's brought us such joy. . . ." Henry's voice broke.

"Mr. Harris, I've stood in your shoes," the doctor said kindly. "I had a baby of my own die. Just about this same age. Picture of health and beauty. Maybe that's the reason this touches me so. But some good came of it. It goaded me on to become a doctor if perchance I could save somebody else's. I might never have made the step save for my own loss."

"I know we're not th' first that ever lost a little one," Hank said. "An' we won't be th' last. But when it's your one an' only, it's. . .hard."

"It's hard on doctors, too." Dr. Murphy turned his head away. "We have to see the starting of life and the ending of it. It. . .it makes you know there's a God."

"Go tell Matthew, Joseph." Somehow it would be easier for Martha if Joseph could be away when the end came. "And please take Effie with you."

When Joseph and Effie returned from The Springs, Sally Rebecca Gibson had departed this life.

177

"It's a dark valley, and you feel that you'll never see a day of happiness again." Pastor Stevens laid a caring hand on Hank's sagging shoulder. "But you will. The sun will shine again in life's cycle of night and day, winter and summer."

Happiness? The world reeled for Joseph. *What is happiness?*

Chapter 21

Tender Feelings

"*I*t comforts me so much that Joseph will be here for th' baby's buryin'," Sarah told Martha. Joseph heard and rearranged his plans to stay for the funeral.

Martha channeled all her motherly instincts into comforting the disconsolate young mother. "There'll be more babies, Sarah," she pointed out. "You're young yet."

"But there'll never be another Rebecca, Mama," Sarah wept.

"No, there'll never be another Rebecca. An' there'll be a tiny little vacant spot forever where she should be, but time will ease the soreness some."

"How. . .how long did the hurt last for Robert?"

"It's still there. . .but it's different. . .not so sharp."

"If'n I could jest put 'er away proper-like," fretted Sarah. "Like a little princess. I don't have nuthin' but cheap flour-sack cotton to line th' coffin Hank's buildin' fer 'er.''

"I have a piece of flannel, but 'tain't th' right color fer a baby."

"My m-mother's w-wedding dress!" Effie patted Sarah's arm. "It's b-beautiful white s-satin and l-lace. U-use it! L-line the c-casket and m-make little R-rebecca a d-dress, too!"

"Oh, no, Effie! I could never think o' takin' yore keepsake and cuttin' it up!" Sarah replied, her heart crushed with grief. "But you're a darlin' to offer it."

"M-my mother would w-want it for R-rebecca, h-her n-namesake."

"But it's yorn, Effie. To keep forever and remember her by."

"P-please."

"Sarah, it's what Effie wants to do for your little angel," Martha supported Effie's decision. "We could make a wonderful smocked satin dress, a tiny pillow, a bonnet, a coverlet, an' have plenty left for linin'. The dress has a long train an' lots an' lots o' lace. Why, she'd be th' prettiest angel ever dressed up to go see God in heaven!"

Sarah smiled through the mist of tears standing in her red, puffy eyes. "Effie, yore th' most unselfishest somebody I ever seen."

"Th-thank you."

"It's you what needs to be said thank you to."

Neither Martha nor Sarah gave in to the necessity of sleep that night. By lamplight, Martha fashioned an elegant dress from the rich bridal satin, smocking the yoke and making tiny lace rosebuds in a row across the front. The intricate puffed sleeves and lacy collar made it a masterpiece of beauty. Then she created a dainty cap, with lace tie strings.

Sarah sat beside her child's body all night with her canvas and paints. "I want to remember her likeness, Mama," she said. "Years will erase my memory if'n I don't make a paintin'." She worked tirelessly hour after hour. The picture of a sleeping child emerged from the bristles of the brush.

Together they lined the box Hank had constructed. Ruffles and pleats of satin sheen formed under artistic fingers. The white pillow under her dark hair made her look like a child peacefully at rest. "She's beautiful!" crooned Sarah. "It makes my heart feel better to lay her away so nice!"

"You can lay 'er in th' churchyard beside our Robert," Martha suggested.

"No, Mama, that's th' Harris plot. I'm a Gibson now, remember. We'll have to start our own row o' graves."

"You're right, Sarah. I keep forgettin'. You 'n Hank's a family o' your own now. That's th' way God meant it to be."

Amy came, mournful and sympathetic, to see the little corpse. Joseph watched as her lips trembled and she choked back the waiting sob. What a pity that a loving young wife like this didn't have her husband here to comfort and support her now. Resentment against his friend Jonathan arose in Joseph's breast, but he conquered it. How Jonathan treated his wife was none of Joseph's concern, he reminded himself once more.

Amy looked up unexpectedly, full into Joseph's observant eyes. He winced. Never had he seen such love and compassion written in deep violet eyes. The sensation of

181

his first encounter with her recycled through his whole being. He wanted to turn and flee, but he was held in a trance-like grip.

"She's as pretty as a picture, isn't she?" Amy spoke scarcely above a whisper, reaching to touch the exquisite dress. "I've never seen a baby dressed so handsomely. She looks like a princess."

"Mother sat up all night making the dress."

"Your mother *made* the dress?"

"Yes. Effie furnished the material. It was her mother's wedding dress."

Martha's wedding dress?

"It's. . .it's perfect."

"Sarah painted her portrait last night. It's a masterpiece."

Amy hung a wreath on the schoolhouse door, closing classes on the day of the funeral. She stood with the Harris family at the graveside service. Somehow she had a feeling of belonging. *Thy people shall be my people, Joseph.*

Pastor Stevens read a verse of Scripture about how "a little child shall lead them" and made his comments. "Little Sally Rebecca Gibson has gone on home ahead of us, leading the way," he said. "The path will be brighter and clearer now and much easier to follow. We will join her someday." He gave the benediction and the family walked slowly away, reluctant to yield the small body to the earth.

"I'll never forget this day as long as I live," Amy said to Joseph. She stood close enough to touch his sleeve. "You have a brave, beautiful family, Joseph. . .excuse me, Mr. Harris."

"Thank you," Joseph turned and left her standing

there. The sentiment proved too much for him. Amy marked it off to grief.

On the final day of Joseph's stay at home, he stopped by the school. "Any more problems?" he asked Amy.

"None, sir. Sandra (she calls herself Sonny) brought word that Claude had decided to quit school. He's three grades behind anyhow. He hasn't been back since the day God sent you to the classroom to rescue me."

"The girl gives no trouble?"

"Sandra may always be Sonny. I hope that I can help her. She flirts with the boys and still uses foul language some, but the boys she trys to impress ignore her. Without Claude as an accomplice, she won't try anything major. I'm. . .I'm actually beginning to like Sandra."

"If you think it's safe, I'll return to my driving job. It's important to. . .Effie that you keep your position."

"If I could convince you that it was unsafe, would you stay?" Merriment brought the dimples.

"Your. . .Mr. Jonathan. . .told me to make sure that you. . .behaved yourself."

Amy gave a short, delightful laugh. "I'll write and tell Jonathan to speak for himself. And if you see him before I do, Mr. Harris, tell him I've decided to finish out the school year here at Brazos Point. I'm enjoying my teaching too much to help him hunt lost relatives. If he can't find them himself. . .well, they'll just have to stay lost! Unless, of course, the school board finds a replacement for me."

"I don't think they're looking for one."

"I hope not."

"I want to thank you personally for what you are doing for Effie."

183

"I need to thank her for what she is doing for me, Mr. Harris. She has the most brilliant mind of any pupil I have ever taught—and a good educational foundation, thanks to you and Dessie."

"And her mother's Bible."

Amy noticed that Joseph kept referring to *her* mother. *Martha Harris's Bible?*

"I have a goal, Mr. Harris. I want you to see a big difference in her speech when you return next time. How long. . .when will. . . ?"

"I may not get back before Spring."

"Spring?"

"Sometimes we get socked in with the winter weather. If I winter at the other end of the line, I can start developing my land."

Why does Amy seem so crestfallen to hear that I be absent during the winter months? Is she afraid of more trouble?

"Just. . .hurry back," she said, blushing. Joseph left more confused than ever.

She was standing beside the road when he drove by on his way westward. He would have sped on, but she raised her hand to detain him. "Will you take this letter to Cousin Grace Browning?" she asked.

"I'd be happy to," he said, taking it from her delicate hand.

"And Godspeed. . .Joseph." She said it tenderly, with feeling, which added to Joseph's discomfort.

Oh, to be on my way to the Territory and shake the net from about my heart! He contemplated the blessed months before his next meeting with this beautiful matron. His heart would have time to forget. . .and heal.

184

Could he have known the contents of the letter he bore
to Grace Browning, his thoughts would have been quite
different. Time and distance could not have kept him from
returning to the young schoolteacher.

Dear Grace

*My heart is doing flip-flops. Joseph, the man
of my dreams has been home for a whole week! At
times, I felt like I was making a mite of progress,
then poof, out would go the light again!*

*Joseph, dear brave Joseph, saved my teaching
position when it was threatened by the school bully, then his lecherous father. It only served to raise
my estimation of him.*

*Death took Sarah's baby and I felt that I would
have given my very life to be able to comfort Joseph
in his grief. Of all the family, I am sure his sorrowing was the loneliest.*

*Effie is doing remarkably well with her stud-
ies. Her speech is slowly improving and she is on
the honor roll. She has taught me more about fortitude and courage than I have taught her in num-
bers and letters.*

*I am yet here for a reason that only God knows.
Sometimes, I think myself a foolish dreamer. If
there's anything you can do for my hopeless cause,
please do it. Joseph thinks the world of you and
Dave.*

*And if my gallivanting brother, Jonathan,
shows up at your place, tell him that my mission
in Texas is not complete. I don't know what it will*

*take to unlock my prince's heart, but I won't give
up until I have tried every key in the bunch.*

> *Hastily (I have to meet him at
> the road as he leaves),*
> *A. Browning*

Chapter 22

Matthew's Exposé

"*I*'ve missed you." Matthew's heart constricted and his throat tightened as he watched Pauline swing slowly back and forth in the grapevine swing, her soft, sweet hands wrapped about the twisted vines.

It was unseasonably warm for November. The maroon leaves, clinging past their appointed lifespan, seemed reluctant to yield themselves to the waiting earth. Or were they held by the grasp of the mother tree dreading the bareness of winter? The sumac bushes, mature and reaching the decline of their annual existence, produced their ultimate of beauty. This was Pauline's favorite season. "Spring is nice and young," she told Matthew, "but maturity brings a special depth in plant life as well as people. Don't you think so? I'll never dread getting old. Older is better!"

Matthew hoped he would never forget the picture she

made today—her long gingham dress falling in billows over her full petticoat, the tips of her pointed shoes barely showing. Her golden hair that fell in stubborn, springy ringlets and her cornflower-blue eyes that contrasted with the backdrop of fall's earthy colors left him heady. This had been their favorite rendezvous for the past three years. "It's almost. . .holy out here," Pauline once said. The cold rushing creek, which paralleled the narrow path they followed to their trysting place, pushed and tumbled over the rocks a short distance away.

Home from college for the Thanksgiving holidays, Matthew had something disturbing his mind; of this Pauline was sure. She read his moods well. His quiet, resolute bearing and decisive air warned her to prepare herself. Patiently, and with trepidation, she waited for his confessional, while he hesitated, adoring the vision of her. He shrank from what he knew he must say, fearing to break love's magic spell.

"I. . .I love you, Pauline, but I'm not sure that you will still want me when my education is complete." Matthew possessed no talent for glib and flowing words. His character was open and honest, his message to the point.

"Whatever can you mean by that, Matthew?" Pauline fought a mounting wave of apprehension. "I'll always want you!" Within she cried, *No! No! Matthew, don't break my heart! I've loved you for three years. I can never care for anyone else like this!*

"There's something like a. . .restlessness. . .digging at my soul. Pauline, I'm not going to be an ordinary preacher. I'm not satisfied with our religion. I plan to search diligently until I find what I'm hungering for—then I'll follow it." He withheld nothing from Pauline. She

188

always listened—and understood.

"Should. . .would that keep you from loving me and me from loving you?"

"No, it wouldn't keep me from loving you. . .or even from marrying you. But you have your parents to consider. Your father's traditions. You are their only child and they have put great stock in you. Possibly I will break with the traditional teachings of our. . .of your father's church."

"I'll be of age on my next birthday, Matthew."

"But you wouldn't want to *disappoint* your family by leaving. . .their church. They have reared you to accept their philosophies."

"But I must choose my own path in life."

"That's my sentiment for myself. There's something deeper for me than. . .formal religion. Inside me is a longing."

"But, Matthew, I've heard Father say the same thing. After a sermon, he tells Mother that he is tired of simply going to church and following a timeworn ritual Sunday after Sunday. He's been restless, too, especially lately. Don't you think that in each of us is that nameless longing that will always be?"

"No, I believe there's a satisfying portion." Matthew sat back on the withered grass, arms encircling his knees, gravely gazing into Pauline's clear questioning eyes. "In my hours of study and prayer, I've made a discovery. Jesus said in the Gospels, 'I am *with* you but I shall be *in* you.' I know that God is *with* me. He has been with me for as long as I can remember. He is with your father. But I want more than that. I want Him *in* me. And there's a vast difference."

189

Pauline stopped swinging and nodded, "Go on!"

"Our religion still knows only the experience in the Gospels, Pauline. God is *with* our church, certainly. I'm not denying that. But that isn't enough. Not until the Book of Acts do we read that Christ was *in* His disciples. We should be living in the experience as recorded in the Book of Acts! We have God 'with us,' but this is not the point of the Gospels, or the rest of the New Testament. The reason Jesus came, lived, died and rose again was so that He could live not only with us but also in us. That is why Jesus told His disciples to return to Jerusalem and receive the Holy Spirit."

"That makes sense, Matthew."

"My roommate and I are in correspondence with some Bible students that have found the Acts 'in you' experience. They are receiving the Holy Ghost—the Comforter that Jesus promised—and speaking with other tongues just as the first believers did on the Day of Pentecost in the Book of Acts, Chapter 2." As Matthew emptied his heart to her, Pauline loved him the more.

"They are even going back to the baptism of the original church, in the name of Jesus. Why don't we? Our own church has veered so far from the pattern the first church left us—miracles, healing, deliverance. We are promised power *in* us when we are born again. I want that experience for myself, Pauline. I'm willing to give up everything, even you, to get it."

"Matthew, when God is *in* us like you're talking about instead of just *with* us, that would be moving closer to Him, wouldn't it? Why should Father, or anyone, object to that?"

"On the surface, it doesn't seem that they would,"

he said slowly, his brown eyes a serious study. "But it changes the whole church dogma and people from almost every denomination are fighting this experience."

"But Father is nondenomination."

"Which would make his position the more precarious because people of all faiths attend our community church and if he should take a positive stand with Peter's message, most of them would resist a Spirit-filled revelation. He'd probably be ousted."

"What about your family, Matthew? Will they protest your new. . .truths?"

"I can't answer that. Mama, especially, is pretty tradition-bound. But my soul's hunger supercedes my fears of family rejection. This gift of the Holy Ghost, Pauline. . .I *want* it. More than I want the approval of my family. . .your family. . .more than I want. . .you. I only hope nothing happens to me before I get this. . .experience. I feel so strongly about it, that I dare not die without it."

"What do you mean by that? You don't. . .plan to die, do you?"

"I don't know. I have a feeling. . .that something might happen."

"I'll stand with you always, Matthew. I want it, too."

"We may have to stand alone."

"No, God will stand with us. If one and God make a majority, what would *two* and God make?"

"You're one in a million!" He got up and stood beside her, offering his hand to lift her from the swing. "Then that's settled. I guess I was afraid. . .you wouldn't understand. I'm relieved."

"I do understand."

191

"I had planned grandly for us, dear. Once my ambition was to land a large church with a substantial income. But with what's burning in my soul, I'll probably have to start my own church—with no income."

"Little is much if God is in it."

"That's right. And I don't read in the Bible where the disciples of Jesus had any earthly possessions."

"As long as we have each other—and God—that's enough for me. He has promised to supply our needs. What more can we ask?"

The couple ambled aimlessly through the woods hand in hand, enjoying the comradeship they felt. The sun shining through the drying leaves cast lacy images all around them. "After today, I love you even more." Matthew lifted her gently over a fallen log.

"Love is like a triangle, Matthew." The glow in Pauline's blue eyes came from deep within. "God is at the top and you and I are across from each other at the bottom. The closer we move to God, the closer we are to each other!"

"Then you'll. . .wait for me?"

"Wait? Matthew, I'd wait a lifetime for you."

"And to think that you started out as my music teacher!"

"And fell in love with my pupil on the very first lesson."

"It was the other way around."

"Teachers make good sweethearts."

"The best."

"Matthew, did Joseph come to see you while he was home?"

"Why, yes, why?"

"Did he mention the new school teacher, Miss Amy?"

"No, I don't recall that he did."

"Miss Amy is smitten with Joseph. And Matthew, they *match*. I'd hoped that he would recognize her quality."

"She's lovely."

"I've never met a sweeter person."

"I don't know what Joseph's problem is."

"I believe he won't *let* himself like her! It's as if he's forcing himself not even to look at her."

"When Joseph came to see me, he seemed lonely."

"He told Miss Amy he probably wouldn't come back until spring. I personally think he's staying away on purpose, and I simply can't figure it out. Surely he can see that her heart is in her eyes for him."

"If he looks in her eyes. I don't know what he's waiting on—or looking for. But I can tell you one thing. Joseph is not happy."

"There's not. . .someone else, is there?"

"Not that I know of."

"He acts as though he's had his heart broken."

"If he's ever been in love, he's kept it a secret from all of us. Now there was a girl in The Territory that got married a few months back, but Joseph didn't show any emotion about it that I could tell."

"You don't think he'd be grieving because Eunice found a beau, do you?"

"No. He told Mama that Eunice seemed like one of the family and he couldn't find it in his heart to be romantic toward her."

"I wish he'd give Miss Amy a chance."

Engrossed in their personal conversation, the brook

drowning out distracting sounds, neither Matthew nor Pauline saw the drunken face of Jake Grimes peering through the brush until he grunted.

Chapter 23

Shot!

"*W*hatya doin' on my place?" Jake Grimes bellowed. "Spyin' on me, ain't ye?" He brandished a rifle, his mouth a river of oaths. The brittle limbs cracked and snapped as he lurched and stumbled forward, the fire of whiskey in his veins.

Matthew took Pauline's arm to hurry her away from the danger, but Jake yelled, "Stop!"

"What is it, Paw?" Claude pushed the brush back, moving up close behind Jake. "Trespassers, huh? We caught 'em, didn't we?"

"Yeah! They're spyin' on us, Claudie! 'Tain't none o' their business what we do on this here property. We rented it fair 'n square, an' this is a free country. A man can make a livin' any way he chooses. Don't have to be no farmer if'n he don't want to. A man can make moonshine if'n he wants to." Jake gave a raucous laugh. "An' we won't have no smart-alecky lovers squealin' on us to th' revenuers neither!''

"I'm sorry, sir. We were just out for a walk. . .and a talk," Matthew attempted to explain. "We. . . ."

"Likely story!" roared Jake. "We know you. You're a Harris. An' a Harris done called th' law on us at th' schoolhouse. We got a score to settle with th' Harrises. An' it might as well be now. Don't you think so, Claudie?"

Matthew backed up, urging Pauline along. "Don't ye move, er I'll shoot," warned the tipsy Jake, black menace in his inflamed eyes. "Th' only way to teach some folks a lesson is to shoot, Claudie," he muttered. "They'll tell if'n we don't get rid o' 'um. I ain't takin' no chances on these kind."

"Wait Paw!" Claude stalled for time. "We could swear 'um to secrecy."

The suggestion didn't work. "They're churchy an' don't swear," Jake reasoned, toying with the trigger on the gun. Matthew motioned frantically behind his back for Pauline to escape, but she refused to leave him.

"Don't shoot, Paw. You might hurt th' pretty girl with th' golden hair. An' pretty girls are hard to come by in these parts. I might be wantin' her fer my bonnie." Claude wanted no bloodshed. And his conscience lacked the callouses of his drunken father.

Matthew impulsively stepped between the raised gun and Pauline.

Jake pawed for the trigger, waving the gun unsteadily.

"Matthew!" screamed Pauline as the shot rang out. Matthew fell to the ground, and Pauline stumbled blindly down the river path toward home, sobbing, calling for

help, and praying as she went.

"Now, look what you done, Paw," shamed Claude. "You killed th' Harris boy an' th' law will be comin' to get you. They'll probably even hang you."

"Well, he oughtn't been spyin' around on my still," defended Jake. "Ain't I got some rights on my own property?" Then Claude's words slowly penetrated his foggy mind. *"Law?* Oh, Claudie, what'll I do? I don't want to go to jail er be hanged fer murder! Oh, Claudie!"

Claude's sympathy awakened. "Aw, Paw, quit yer blubberin'! When th' law comes, I'll swear on a stack o' Bibles it was a pure accident. I was an eyewitness, remember. Th' only other one that saw th' killin' was th' pretty girl, an' I can shut 'er up quick, I promise. Girls ain't hard to spook. So don't worry no more."

They backed away from the motionless body on the ground into the woods. At a safe distance, Jake whispered, "Best thing fer us to do, Claudie, is pack our duds an' get out o' here today! Come on!" He ran unsteadily toward the barn dwelling with Claude in close pursuit. "Hurry it up, Claudie!"

Claude stifled a choking fear, remembering the big man that collared him in the schoolhouse. *It might be best to clear out, all right,* he thought.

"Pack up, Maw, and let's get out o' here soon's it gets good dark. Sonny, help yer maw pack up an' be quick about it."

"What's th' big hurry, Jake?" Mrs. Grimes asked, surprised at his furtive over-the-shoulder glances toward the river. "Are th' revenuers on our trail a'ready? We hain't been here but. . . ."

"Paw killed one o' th' Harris bunch, Maw. He was

197

trespassin' on our place an' spyin' on Paw's still. Paw shot 'im dead."

"Jake! You didn't!"

"They'll never find us."

"Why, Jake, we don't even have a wagon."

"Take what ye can on yer back an' leave th' rest," demanded Jake, rattled. "We ain't got nuthin' that matters nohow. I'll git ye another fryin' pan."

"I ain't helpin' pack nuthin!" sulked Sonny.

"You'll do as I say, an' not be so sassy." Jake struck at her, but she dodged.

"I don't like this way o' life. Always runnin'," she griped. "'Bout th' time I get to likin' my teacher an' learnin', I get jerked up an' moved somewhere else. I'm tired o' it!"

"Well, you sure don't want yer paw goin' to jail fer murder, do you?" Claude shouted.

"I don't care where he goes! Sometimes I think we'd be better off if'n he did!" she retaliated. "Then we could stay in one place an' learn to get along with people. Miss Amy told me I could be a nice young lady if I half try. I wanted to tell her I would if'n I had half th' chance! I'm tired o' bein' a bootlegger's daughter! I want to go to church, an' have friends an'. . . ."

"We shoulda left afore now, Paw," Claude said. "See how Sonny has done got near brainwashed by that woman teacher? Thinkin' th' teacher knows better'n her paw. Hain't that shameful?"

"I knowed that teacher was no 'count."

"I think it's time we move on regardless o' th' shootin', Paw. Th' nicey-nicey churchgoin' schoolteacher done got Sonny wantin' to be like regular people! An' we ain't cut out by that pattern! Nosiree!''

"I'm not Sonny, I'm Sandra!" Sonny blurted angrily. ''An' I don't want to go to another new place an' pretend I'm tough when I'm really cryin' inside for friends like other girls has got! I want to stay here with Miss Amy!''

"Sonny's talkin' nonsense now, Maw. Hurry up yer packin'. Let's get 'er out o' here!" But Sonny had turned and fled.

Amy treadled the antiquated organ, the pedals worn thin in a foot-shaped pattern corresponding with the size of Sister Myrt's large feet. She enjoyed the solitude of the church at this Thanksgiving season, assuring herself that she had much to be thankful for. She was counting her blessings when she heard the front door creak open cautiously. Sonny stood there crying. Her bare legs, accustomed to her brother's trousers, shone white beneath her too-short dress.

"Why, Sandra! What's wrong, dear?" Amy swiveled the stool around to face the weeping girl. "Stop crying and tell me!"

"I don't exactly know what happened, Miss Amy. I think Paw hurt somebody bad or somethin'. He's drunk again—an' he says we must move away tonight! An', oh, Miss Amy, I love you an' I don't want to move away. You're th' best teacher I ever had. You're th' only one that ever *cared* about me. It always happens. Paw's always runnin'.''

Amy arose and put her arms about the sorrowing girl. "Sandra," she said, moved with pity, "something tells me that the good you have inside of you will soon surface wherever you are. I'm sorry to lose you from my class, but you will have to go with your parents, of course. You're not yet of age. But I do have a suggestion."

"What is it, Miss Amy?"

"Start out at the next place by being a real lady. You can overcome your circumstances, however terrible. You don't have to prove anything, Sandra. If you'll be yourself, people will like you for what you are. Just be your own sweet self. And someday perhaps we'll meet again and I'll be proud of what you've made of yourself!"

"I'm from good stock, Miss Amy. Honest, I am. My grandpa is a preacher. Paw was th' black sheep. Grandpa says Paw is runnin' from God. An' he may be right, too."

"That's possible."

"I want to be just like you, Miss Amy! I never wanted to be bad. It's just hard, not havin' no friends nowhere I went. I don't get close to nobody, cause I live in fear they'll find out Paw is a bootlegger. You knew that, didn't you, Miss Amy?"

"Why, no, I didn't, Sandra. But it wouldn't have made any difference in the way I felt about you if I had."

"Honest, it wouldn't?"

"No, it wouldn't. I would have been all the prouder of you for trying so hard. But I see how difficult it would be for a young lady. I tell you what we need to do. Let's kneel here in the church and ask God to go with you and help you. We won't have to tell anybody about our prayer."

Sonny fell to her knees and Amy prayed a touching prayer. Sonny looked small and innocent beside her, a "sheep among wolves." But she got up smiling. "Just keep prayin' for me, Miss Amy. An' I'll try my very best to be good." Then Sonny slipped out the door and was gone from Amy's life.

Now it was Amy's turn to weep. *You never know what's inside a child's heart,* she thought. *Days like today make teaching worth the effort. I'll miss Sonny—Sandra. Like her name, she's a paradox.*

Amy returned to the organ and her blessing—counting, playing softly and meditating reflectively on her almost three months in this small hamlet. *Yes, I will miss Sonny, the hard shell with the soft middle. Who has Jake Grimes "hurt"? Why the mad rush to get out of the area? Jake Grimes, the bootlegger.*

Amy evaluated her other pupils. *There is Pauline, who will be graduating in May—soft, gracious, polite. She is just right for a "preacher's wife," with an undying love for Matthew Harris. There is a couple who will do great things for God's kingdom. It has been a joy to teach Pauline, and in return Pauline has taught me some things about life. Teaching is a two-way street. One gives, but one also receives. Pauline is an only child, yet unspoiled and unspoilable. . . .Dare I hope that someday Pauline will be my own sister-in-law?*

Effie is making amazing progress with her speech. . . .

"*Miss Amy!*" Mrs. Stevens bolted through the door, pale and frightened. Amy jumped up, gathering her skirts about her. "Matthew's been shot!" Mrs. Stevens cried.

"Matthew Harris? *Shot?*" Sonny's words rang in Amy's ears: "Paw's drunk. . .I think he hurt somebody bad. . .we have to leave tonight. . . ." *Oh, no!* "What happened, Sister Stevens?"

"We don't know. Pauline is hysterical. Please come, Miss Amy!"

Chapter 24

Letter to Jonathan

*N*o amount of persuasion could keep Pauline from returning to the scene of the shooting with her father. She set her face as a flint.

"Father might not be able to find him," she told her mother, and she led the way valiantly. Matthew lay as she had left him.

"Matthew!" Pastor Stevens knelt beside the still form of the young man on a bed of drab, fallen leaves. Hot tears fell from the parson's chin onto Matthew's shirt. "Matthew, can you hear me?" Pauline stood a stone's throw away, wringing her hands helplessly.

Pastor Stevens pressed Matthew's jugular vein, feeling for a heartbeat. The body was still warm.

Matthew slowly opened his eyes. "Are they gone?" he whispered.

"They're gone," the pastor answered tersely.

"Tell Pauline I'm not hurt badly," Matthew spoke quietly.

"Praise God!" rejoiced Brother Stevens. "Pauline, he's alive!" Pauline edged closer, hardly daring to believe the hallowed words of her father.

"Mr. Grimes was too drunk to shoot straight." Matthew's voice gained volume. "The bullet barely grazed my shoulder. But I feared if I moved, he'd shoot again. And the second shot might be a little more accurate."

Pastor Stevens helped Matthew to his feet and brushed off his clothes. Pauline, oblivious to her father's presence, impulsively flung her arms around her beloved, sobbing. "Oh, Matthew, Matthew!" was all she could say. "I thought I had lost you!" Pastor Stevens modestly pretended to study some object at a distance until the embrace was over.

"What happened, Matthew?" he then queried. "I'm afraid Pauline was too shook up to tell us much."

Matthew managed a shaky laugh. "The best I can figure, we got too close to Mr. Grimes's still."

"Still?"

"Yes. He's evidently been bootlegging whiskey here and he thought Pauline and I were spying on him."

"Well, a few things add up now. Bootlegging, huh?"

"I'm ready to get away from here!"

"We'll have to notify the county sheriff, Matthew."

"I. . .it's over now. . .and we can just forget it."

"No, Matthew. This isn't the first trouble the man has created for our community. If we let him get by with this, he'll try something else. Someone eventually will be killed."

"Still. . .I'd rather leave vengeance in the hands of

God."

"That's what peace officers are for. I think we should file charges."

"I. . .I guess I. . .we were trespassing."

"Trespassing? Along the *riverbed?* On unfenced property? The land doesn't belong to Jake Grimes anyhow!"

"What would we charge him with?"

"Bootlegging and intent to murder."

The trio returned to the parsonage, but Pastor Stevens saddled up his horse immediately and left for town.

When the sheriff arrived, accompanied by the clergyman, the barn where the Grimes had lived was cluttered with debris and the Grimeses were gone. Only the smell of fermented fruit remained as telltale evidence.

"Looks like he eluded us," the sheriff said. "Shall we put a tracer on him? You want to sign a complaint?"

The pastor was pensive. "No," he said finally. "We'll just thank God that no one was killed. The man's gone. . .and it's a blessed riddance for our community."

With a four-day recess from teaching, Amy sat down and wrote to Jonathan.

Dear Brother

I thought I was coming to an uneventful country village to be a quiet old-maid school teacher. Boy, was I ever fooled! If I had it to do over—you guessed it—I'd do it again!

As to your offer to send me a ticket to join you, I must tell you that I am content here for now. You can, however, send me some extra money (would

I be a sister if I didn't ask for more money?) to buy Christmas gifts for Joseph's family and for the Stevens family where I live.

Our Thanksgiving holidays were almost marred by a tragedy. The local bootlegger shot at Joseph's younger brother, Matthew, barely missing. Now don't come swooping down to rescue me from a rough, rowdy society! The culprit moved his family to an unknown destination in his fright. He was the community's only "bad apple."

Out of the seed of malice blossomed a beautiful flower for me. The bootlegger's daughter, my "problem child"—a tough, irreverent girl of fifteen—made an about-face and paid me the highest of compliments. She will develop into a worthy citizen, an honor to me and her country.

As I talked with her, I wished for a home of my own. I would have taken Sandra (her family calls her Sonny) to live with me. Behind her bravado hides a heart of aching loneliness. I hope to meet her again someday.

You cannot believe the progress that Effie, Joseph's crippled sister, is making in school. The child amazes me! She stuttered terribly when I first came, but her speech has improved impressively. She has the most beautiful attitude I have ever found in a child, and the prettiest crooked smile God ever put on a human face. I am already dreading the thought of leaving her at school's end.

Dear brother, teaching is the most rewarding thing I've ever done. When I hear my smaller ones pledge allegiance to the flag of the United States and see their little hands over their hearts, an emotion wells up inside me, making me want to both laugh and cry for joy. The nations' destiny rests on these youngsters. They are our future.

Joseph lost a little niece six weeks ago—the most darling baby I have ever seen. She had black ringlets and they dressed her in a handmade white satin dress for burial. She looked like a princess. Joseph was here for the funeral.

I gave Joseph the papers you sent (in person). He seemed overjoyed about the papers and he thinks they will enable him to get the land he has his heart set upon. I told him that you would give him the details of his uncle's death on your return trip. He accepted the news calmly, having reconciled himself to this possibility years ago.

The bite of the drought in Central Texas hasn't lessened. Frankly, I don't see how large families like the Harrises are making ends meet. The funds I pay the Stevenses for my room and board are helping keep them afloat, for which I am grateful.

The Stevenses have a beautiful daughter, Pauline, but Matthew found her first. You're out of luck on this one, I'm afraid. She is madly in love with Matthew and they plan to be married when he finishes college. If romance was contagious, I'd surely catch it here!

I guess I'll remain a spinster. No one else interests me since I met Joseph, the coach driver and heart rustler.

Are you having any better luck in your search for Aunt Annie? I do plan to finish out the school

*year here even if you locate her prior to that time.
You know me, I don't like unfinished projects. That
is, unless the school board finds a replacement for
me, and Joseph assured me that they weren't
looking.*

   *I am making no progress with the coach. . .and
I'm about ready to say "never."*

Your loving sister,

Amy B.

Amy folded the letter and addressed the envelope in
care of Mrs. Bimski. Then she pulled out another tablet
sheet and began her Christmas list. *Dare I secretly embrace the Harris family as "my family"? Or is this
schoolgirl daydreaming? I could bring about my own
heartbreak by foolish fancies. I am too intelligent for that.
Or am I?*

   To crowd out further soul-searching that was leaving her vaguely discomfited, she turned her thoughts to
the Christmas activities she planned for her classroom.
Miss Vivian didn't hold with holiday festivity and a tree
in the schoolhouse would be a novel experience for the
Brazos Point scholars. A tree in the "place of learning"
was unheard of! Amy had found several things that Miss
Vivian didn't hold with and deemed it best to ease slowly
away from the sterile, cut-and-dried mold of the past into her own young ideas.

   Her plan this season was to entice those parents who

208

separated home and school as rigidly as Pastor Stevens separated church and state to come to the school program. A scene from Luke's story of the birth of Jesus could be accomplished with a bit of practice. Pauline would read the story text while the younger children portrayed the unforgettable characters. William would be a shepherd, as well as Jesse Gibson.

Amy breathed a sigh of relief. The Grimeses would not be here to create a disturbance. *Would I have been brave enough to formulate plans which included the parents of my students had Jake Grimes still been on the loose?*

And what about Effie? The program would be incomplete without my star pupil. Of course! She'll be an angel—with her bent wings folded out of sight under her glistening white costume. Heaven itself couldn't produce a more suitable cherub.

Amy's mind churned with details. *There will be sacks of candy and nuts for everyone. I will see to that myself. The room will be decorated with boughs of greenery, holly berries, mistletoe. Have I ever had such fun planning anything?*

Pastor Steven's mother was aging and ailing, so the Stevenses took a trip into Cleburne. The visit was on a Saturday and Mrs. Stevens invited Amy to go along and "see the growing town," which was the county seat of Johnson County. Knowing that funds from Jonathan would be forthcoming, Amy took her ample cash reserve and blessed her luck for a day of Christmas shopping. She removed her shopping list from her pocket and reviewed it:

Matthew – briefcase

William – chess game
Dessie – vanity set
The President's Boys – metal banks filled with Indian head pennies
Sally – doll
Effie – fleecy robe
Mr. Harris – French harp
Mrs. Harris – bedroom slippers
Pauline – parasol
Pastor Stevens – Bible reference book
Mrs. Stevens – handbag
Yes, gifts and personalities matched. How I wish that I might include Joseph on my list!

Chapter 25

Effie's Promise

"*M*iss Amy, you have a bug in your hair!"

Amy shook her head and swatted at her hair to rid herself of the insect.

"April fool!"

The class took full advantage of the first day of April, their youthful mirth running rampant. They had teased her all afternoon.

A dry, cold winter had passed with not a word from Joseph. Now the calendar proclaimed April. "Joseph's here, Miss Amy!"

Another April fool prank. This is the last. . .and worst of the day. Amy gave Jesse Gibson the signal to pull the bell rope. *Thank God, April Fool's Day only comes once a year!*

The children filed out in an orderly way, a lesson she had finally gotten across to them. And when the last one exited, with only Effie left for an oral test, Joseph stepped in the door, hat in hand.

"If I may have a minute of your time. . ." he bowed.

"Surely. As much time as you wish, Mr. . . .Harris."

"I've. . .I've promised Effie a trip to The Territory while I'm yet driving the stage." Joseph appeared eager to get to the heart of the matter and be finished with it. "And I may not be driving much longer. I have a freight haul to make to Amarillo and would like to take her with me if she could be spared from her schooling for about six weeks."

Amy caught the rapture in Effie's pixie face, the pleading in her eyes, and could not possibly deny the child this trip. "How lovely!" she said. "A vacation!"

"I want to take her while it's still cool."

"I see no harm in her absence from school, Mr. Harris. She's advanced beyond her grade level already. A few weeks away won't hinder her promotion to the next grade."

"Thank you, kindly. I wish to take her to Caprock to meet the Brownings and visit her mother's grave."

"Her. . .mother's grave? I thought. . .I thought Effie was your sister."

"My adopted sister," Joseph smiled, his eyes on the wall beyond her. "She was born in the Territory to Uncle Charles and Aunt Rebecca, and her mother is buried there. I suppose that's one reason the land holds a special appeal for me."

"I see. How long has Effie been. . .your sister?"

"Since she was three."

"You were born in that beautiful country?" The indentions began in Amy's glowing cheeks. "Why, Effie!

212

How wonderful of Joseph. . .uh, Mr. Harris, to take you to visit your birthplace! And you'll get to meet the Brownings!"

"Yes!" Effie beamed. "I've a-always wanted to go th-there!" Joseph was taken aback. Effie scarcely stuttered at all!

"Have you had word from your. . .Mr. Jonathan lately?" Joseph asked Amy out of courtesy.

"Yes, sir. He's about ready to give up the search as a lost cause. He's coming to visit me around the first of June and I suppose we'll be returning at that time to 'the Old Kentucky Home' as the song goes."

"The students will miss you next year—if you don't choose to return."

"And I'll miss them—especially Effie!"

Joseph sat, somewhat uncomfortably, and waited while Amy gave Effie her world history test. The music in the teacher's voice reverberated through his soul. He studied the flower arrangement on her desk as a distraction. Effie answered every question without hesitancy. Pride swelled in his heart. *What an advancement Effie has made in my absence!*

Effie got stiffly to her feet. "I'll see you w-when I return!" She waved to Amy, then took Joseph's hand.

Amy locked the door and walked to the parsonage, now convinced that it was "never" for her and Joseph as she had written Jonathan. To talk with her actually seemed a distasteful chore for him!

"Mother, we need to leave tomorrow so I can have Effie back for the school promotions the end of May," Joseph urged, plunging Martha into flurried preparations for Effie's departure. Then Joseph turned to Henry.

"You've had a little rainfall?" he asked.

"Some scattered thundershowers that kicked up the dust, but not enough to pay the moisture debt left owing by last year's heat. And the winter was dry—no snow, no ice to quench the earth's thirst."

"What about this year's crops?"

"I fear for them. I've planted, but they're not prosperin'. Your maw is worryin' herself sick."

William entered the conversation to share the homefront news. "Guess what, Joseph? Since th' Grimeses moved, I'm catchin' catfish again! We're havin' fish for supper!"

"An' we're gettin' milk again," Dessie added.

"An' we don't have to worry about gettin' shot!" Henry chuckled. "It's dangerous, havin' a bootlegger for a neighbor."

"They didn't give your schoolteacher any more trouble did they, William?" Joseph queried.

"Nope. Claude quit school, an' Sonny got almost plumb nice to ever'body before they left. Teacher would have made a perfect lady out o' her if'n she'da stayed."

"But she never quit winkin' at you, William!" Dessie reminded.

"Well. . . ."

"You shoulda been here Christmas, Joseph!" Chester broke in, face alight with exciting memories. "Teacher bought us all th' *nicest* Christmas things—besides fruit an' candy. We had th' best time, didn't we, Papa? She must be *rich!*"

"She got me an' Alan an' Chester toy banks *filled* with Indian head pennies," Arthur supplied. "I still got mine."

"And I got a b-beautiful r-robe!" Effie said. "Mother's

214

p-packing it now."

"Miz Amy even got me an' Mama a gift," Henry said. "She's like one o' th' family. We'll miss her somethin' dreadful when she goes back to Kentucky."

"She tells me that her. . ." (Joseph had never been able to bring himself to say "husband") ". . .Mr. Jonathan is coming back in June."

"I'm afraid so."

"And I'm afraid I'll c-cry," Effie said. "I l-love her."

"The good Lord will send you another teacher," promised Joseph.

"There'll never be a-another M-miss Amy!"

Mrs. Amy, corrected Joseph, but not aloud. *And you're right, there'll never be another.*

"Will you go on to see Jim and Charlotte, Joseph?" Dessie questioned.

"If all goes well, I want to take Effie to Santa Fe."

"Oh, g-goody!"

"Time will be the deciding factor. We'll hurry like fury to get in all the sightseeing we can, won't we, Effie?"

"Oh, yes!"

Effie had a difficult time going to sleep. Dessie needed little urging to share her room that night, and the hum of their excited voices hung in the air long after the lamps had gone out.

"Just think, D-dessie. I'll get to see w-where I was b-born!"

"An' you'll get to meet Jim's wife!"

"And I'll g-get to see an I-Indian Joseph said J-Jim has as his h-housekeeper."

"I wish I could go, too," Dessie said wistfully.

"But you h-have to stay in s-school."

215

"Yes. Miss Amy wouldn't like both of us to miss."

"You'll get to g-go s-someday. When J-Joseph moves out th-there."

"I was hopin' Joseph would marry Miss Amy an' take her with him to th' Territory."

"He still m-might."

"He'd better hurry! Miss Amy's leavin' when school's out. An' we'll probably never see her again!"

Effie yawned. "K-keep her here till we g-get back. . .and I'll have J-Joseph liking her by th-then!"

After breakfast the following morning, Joseph lifted Effie onto the top seat of the coach, stowed her clothing away and signaled the horses to trot amid waving, cheers, and Martha's tears.

Amy left the manse earlier than usual. She wished to be alone with her thoughts and the day begged recognition. A gentle breeze patted her face and the brisk walk renewed her spirits. A glossy dew kissed the just emerging bluebonnets. As she turned the key in the schoolhouse door, she heard the thud of hooves. Pausing in the shade of the giant live oak tree, she watched the handsome coach with its heart-stopping cargo sweep by. Perhaps it was more than mere happenstance that brought her to school early that day.

Effie waved her crippled hand merrily and Joseph tipped his hat solemnly, not bothering to turn his head in her direction.

Chapter 26

The Revelation

"*M*iss Amy thinks you're h-handsome, Joseph."

A whole day lay behind the travelers when Effie brought up her favorite subject, remembering her promise to Dessie. The scenic route coupled with her keen perception and pleasure had kept her mind occupied during the trip's infancy.

"You have a very nice teacher, Effie. I'm proud of the progress you have made."

"Thank you."

"She has a handsome husband, too."

"*H-husband?*"

"Yes, I've met him. I took him to the train near Santa Fe just before. . .your teacher came to Brazos Point."

"Miss A-Amy doesn't *h-have* a husband!"

"His name is Mr. Jonathan Browning, Effie. I'm sure he is proud of Amy, too." *Although I don't understand*

217

his long absence from her.

"Mr. J-Jonathan is Miss Amy's *b-brother!* He's gone to C-California to find some l-lost relatives to s-settle in a s-state."

Joseph laughed. "To settle *an estate,*" he corrected. "And then he'll return for his wife and they'll go back to their home in Kentucky."

"No! No! Miss Amy t-told me all about her b-brother. He's two years older than she is. Th-they're the only two in the f-family and their p-parents are dead. L-like my mother. You've seen her b-brother? D-do they f-favor?"

Joseph thought. *Their eyes. They have the same eyes!* But he dared not hope that Effie was correct. He delved into his memory trying to recall if Jonathan had actually said that Amy was his wife or if he had merely jumped to conclusions. *I can't afford to let myself in for a disappointment,* he argued, but in spite of himself, the possibility brought a heart-quickening thrill. *Suppose Amy isn't married! Suppose. . .oh, the faintest thought of it is too wonderful!*

"You're quite sure Miss Amy is single, Effie?"

"Oh, I'm p-positive, J-Joseph! She said she g-guessed she'd never get m-married! She's nearly twenty-two and she d-doesn't even have a b-beau!"

"I'm glad. . .I mean, I'm surprised. She's so. . .different from most young ladies her age. Her values are. . .deeper." Joseph felt his face grow red. The new revelation had him flustered. "Very unspoiled and unselfish. Conscientious, too."

"W-why did you think she was m-married, Joseph?"

"I'm trying to remember. The first time I saw her, Jonathan brought her a drink of water and helped her onto the coach—as any husband would do."

"Couldn't a b-brother do that? Wouldn't you d-do that for me? If he w-was a nice b-brother like you, he w-would. And I'm sure J-Jonathan is a nice b-brother."

"Why, yes, I guess so. Then. . .then I thought that Mr. Browning at Caprock was *Jonathan's* cousin, but not Miss Amy's. Everything seems pretty mixed up in my mind now that I think back. I just took for granted from the start that they were married, them traveling together and all."

"And so th-that's why you wouldn't give Miss Amy a c-chance to be your s-sweetheart. . .'cause you th-thought she was m-married?" Effie squirmed with excitement.

That Effie! She has a way of delving deep into a person's soul. "That's likely the reason."

"A-and that's why you wouldn't l-look at her w-when you talked to her?"

Perceptive kid. "Perhaps so."

Effie laughed, a sweet, bubbly sound. "S-since you found out she's not r-really married after all, w-will she be your s-sweetheart now?"

"I'm afraid if I ever convince myself that I've been wrong, I'll be a slave to her charms. She's the loveliest young lady I've ever met."

"Oh, g-goody!"

Still unwilling to give rein to the impatient tugging of his heart, Joseph held his emotions at bay. *In the mouth of two or three witnesses. . .* He wanted desperately not to doubt Effie, but this matter was far too important to rest on a child's word. He knew he must be rational, realizing that a slip of a girl could confuse fact and fiction in

219

the trappings of life. To admit hope as a guest into the chambers of his soul was too risky. His very heart was at stake.

The logical thing to do, he decided, would be to divert his mind, an almost impossible task, until he could confirm Effie's disclosure. *Be still, heart.*

His mind groped about for an egress. He looked right and left for a mental diversion. The flat, panhandle plains glared back at him emptily. Then he thought of a story Jim had told him on his first trip west. Thinking of it made other thoughts sit quietly in the background.

"Jim told me a story your father shared with him about this part of the country."

"P-please tell me!" Effie urged, never tiring of history concerning her family.

"Let's name the story 'The Wicked Villain.'"

"Okay!"

"Charles and Rebecca camped hereabouts one night. The weather was hot so they pulled their pallets out onto the ground beside the wagon. During the night, a fresh south wind stirred, sweeping under the wagon to cool them. Rebecca awoke with a start and saw a large, dark object moving toward the wagon. It bent close to the ground, hovering ominously."

"Ooooooo," shivered Effie, engrossed in the tale. "Go o-on."

"Rebecca watched it beneath the wagon as it crouched and moved closer. 'Charles!' she whispered—and the thing paused. Had it heard her? Then it came on a few paces at a run, halting again. Was it an Indian? A wild animal? A bandit? 'Charles, wake up!' She shook him, crying."

Joseph embellished the story with dramatics.

"Hurry, J-Joseph! You're g-going too slow!"

"Charles bolted upright and reached for his gun. 'Where?' he asked. 'On the other side of the wagon, trying to slip up on us!' Charles didn't want to shoot. 'I've never shot anything before,' he told Rebecca, 'but I have to protect you.' "

"S-so?"

"The thing was just a few yards beyond the wagon now. 'Halt!' ordered Charles. It stopped for a moment, then inched forward very carefully, finally breaking into a wild run toward them. Rebecca screamed and Charles shot. But the shot didn't stop their enemy. 'I missed,' Charles gasped and shot again at close range. Still the villain didn't flinch, but hid behind the wagon's rear wheel and refused to budge from his hiding place. 'I think I've injured him, Rebecca,' Charles said and eased around the wagon to see. Whatever it was made no sound. Rebecca was praying, 'Oh, God, don't let Charles get hurt or killed. What would I do out here in no-man's land by myself?' "

The suspence tantalized Effie while Joseph enjoyed dragging out the plot. "Then Charles called to her. 'Come see what we wasted a couple of good bullets on.' "

"W-what was it?"

"A tumbleweed! Like that one coming yonder." Joseph pointed toward the massive brown weed tumbling end over end.

"Tumblew-weeds?"

"That's what they are called. Tumbleweeds are funny plants. They grow for a year, then cut themselves loose from the ground and go rolling across the country, spreading seeds as they go. It's God's way of planting more tumbleweeds."

"I l-love the s-story."

"I knew you would." *And I enjoyed it, too,* Joseph told himself. *I've gone for a whole thirty minutes without thinking about Amy!*

"T-tell me more about my m-mother and f-father."

"Your father had some witty little sayings. One I especially liked. He said there were two kinds of tongues—wagon tongues and waggin' tongues—and that the length of both were about the same."

Effie giggled. "P-pretty good, huh?"

"And pretty true. He claimed that he went to The Territory to get away from waggin' tongues."

"Is that why you're g-going?"

Joseph chuckled. "No."

"Do you th-think my father is d-dead, Joseph?" Effie asked. As Joseph had feared, the question came unexpectedly. He had planned to wait for Jonathan's details before breaking the news to her.

"We know he is now, Effie." He knew Effie would want it straight from the shoulder. "Jonathan learned about his death in California. I have the papers on his land. When Amy's hus. . .Jonathan comes back from his trip, he will tell us all about your father and how he met his death."

Effie was quiet for a long while, sorting out her grief. When she spoke, it was not about her father.

"You almost forgot that J-Jonathan is Amy's b-brother and not her h-husband, didn't you?"

"Almost."

"Y-you don't quite b-believe me, do you?"

"Not quite."

Effie laughed. "You're the d-doubtingest someb-body

222

I ever saw! But you'll f-find out the t-truth. . .then you'll m-marry her!''

Chapter 27

Successes and Failures

"*I* never dreamed that I would miss Effie so dreadfully!" Amy told Pauline as they walked to school together, pausing on the iron-ribbed bridge to look into the clear water of the Brazos River below, listening to its liquid melody. "I realize now that my motivating reason for coming to teach was to help her, after I heard Joseph say she had never attended a public school. Now that she's gone. . .I'll actually be glad when school is out."

"Effie's a brave girl." Pauline watched a fish fight its way upstream, comparing it with Effie's struggle against life's odds. "She lived under miserable circumstances until a year and a half ago."

"Did these circumstances also affect. . .Joseph?"

"Very much."

"Grace Browning mentioned that Joseph had been burdened with family problems. She didn't go into detail."

"Had it not been for Joseph, Effie probably would not have survived. He championed her cause from the start. He gave her the courage to go on living."

"What do you mean by that, Pauline?"

"When Effie's mother died and Charles Harris, Mr. Harris's younger brother, brought Effie here, Martha Harris was ashamed of her. She was of the old school that believed people with disabilities were demon-possessed."

"How tragic!"

"Yes, it was. She tried to hide Effie from society. We didn't know about her for months and months! Papa finally got wind of her existence through the head deacon's wife, who had a very long tongue. She had been to visit Martha and discovered Effie there. She got the story all confused and told Papa that Effie was an illigitmate child born to Martha Harris. When Papa went to investigate, Sister Harris hid Effie in the pantry. We learned the truth from Matthew. It was pitiful. Joseph and Dessie taught her to walk, talk, and read. Joseph even made corncob dolls for her on Christmas so she wouldn't feel so left out. He treated her like a human."

"How did the change take place? Mrs. Harris treats her almost with partiality now! One would never know that she ever discriminated against her."

"We were all praying. Martha Harris was making plans to put Effie away in an asylum against Joseph's wishes. Then came a near tragedy. I'm sure it was God's doings. Effie risked her own life to save Little Sally from a fire a year ago last October. The baby's wicker baby carriage caught aflame from a coal from under the washpot. Martha had taken an armload of dried clothes inside. Since then, I'm sure Sister Harris feels she owes

Effie a great deal."

"Do you think Joseph will take Effie to live with him when he gets mar. . .makes a home of his own? He's awfully crazy about her."

"Martha Harris wouldn't hear of it!"

"Have you noticed, Pauline, that Martha Harris doesn't look well lately?" Amy propped her sun-kissed arms on the bridge rails. "I spoke to her at church Sunday and she said she had been ill all week."

"Dessie tells me she's still sick."

"She seems worried about something. You don't think it's Effie, do you?"

"No, I don't believe she would worry about Effie as long as she is in Joseph's custody. I believe there's something else bothering Sister Harris."

"I. . .I'll bake her a butter pound cake and take over this afternoon."

"I've heard of feeding the goose to get the gander," teased Pauline mischievously.

"If I thought that would work, I'd bake her a cake every day!"

A letter awaited Amy when she returned to the parsonage after school. The slanted cursive was familiar. *Where have I seen it? At school, that's where!* It was Sandra Grimes's handwriting, penned fastidiously on expensive stationery. *What a lovely surprise!*

Dear Miss Amy

So much has happened since our prayer! Paw was killed in a barroom brawl. Shot in cold blood in a drunken stupor. Claude says he got into an

227

argument about his brew being better than the bour-
bon served by the bartender. He was trying to steal
some of the bartender's customers by bragging on
his own grog. He got mad when a customer contradicted him and he started a fight.

Paw never found his way to God, it sorrows
me to tell you. It was a great grief to Grandpa who
had prayed many prayers for his salvation. But
if Paw had lived a lifetime, I don't think he would
ever have changed. He got even more hard and bitter after we left there.

Maw sent me to live with Grandma and
Grandpa after Paw was buried, and I have a great
life here. Grandma showed me how to curl my hair
like a lady and made me a silk dress with a gathered skirt and bow sash. I feel like a queen! You
would be proud of me, Miss Amy. Grandpa and
Grandma are trying to raise me by the Bible.

And guess what? The most gorgeous boy in
Grandpa's church is trying to claim me as his bonnie. I'm playing hard to get, though. That makes
him try all the harder to get my attention. But
don't worry, I'll give him just enough encouragement so he won't give up!

Maw is on charity now, but Claude promised
to get a job on the railroad and support her when
he turns eighteen next month. Claude is changing,
but real slowly. I'm not glad Paw died, Miss Amy.
That would be wicked. But I'm glad for a chance
at a better life. It must all be a part of God's plan.

Claude told me about Paw shooting Matthew,
and I can't sleep at night for thinking about it.

*Could you tell Pauline that I'm terrible sorry?
Claude thought Paw killed Matthew, but he wasn't
for sure.*

*I am very embarrassed when I think of the way
I acted at Brazos Point. I wish I could erase that
chalkboard of my past and start with a clean slate.
But it was worth everything having you for my
teacher. I have a good teacher and many friends
here, and I am doing well in school, but my teacher
is not **special** like you.*

*You will be happy to know that I am planning
on going to college to become a schoolteacher myself.
Grandpa will supply my tuition. I hope that I may
be able to help a "Sonny" like you helped me.*

Love,

Sandra Grimes

Amy shared her letter with the Stevenses, and
Pauline reached for a handkerchief to staunch her tears.

"You just never know, do you?" Pastor Stevens shook
his head in amazement. "Miss Amy, that child will be a
star in your crown!"

"I can say I've been well rewarded for taking the
teaching position here. Do you know, we're in the last
six weeks and I believe every one of my pupils will pass
this year!"

"Will you consider returning to teach for us next
year?" Brother Stevens had planned for several days to

broach the subject. "The job is yours if you'll take it. I'll see if I can get you a raise in salary."

"No, Pastor, I don't think I'll accept the teaching term for next year. I've given it a good deal of thought, but I don't feel it. . .here." Amy placed her hand on her heart. "I suppose Jonathan and I will return to the homeplace. I really don't know what God has in mind for my life in the future. Sometimes I wish I did. Then other times, it's probably best I don't."

"I'd try a little persuasion if it would help," the pastor urged. "It will be quite impossible to replace you."

"Thank you. It's nice to be wanted, but my mission here is fulfilled."

Left alone with Mrs. Stevens in the kitchen, Amy sighed. "I've won some battles and lost some." She blended the melted butter into her flour and sugar mixture for Martha's cake. "But that's life, isn't it?"

Mrs. Stevens knew what Amy meant. "You don't think given time—another year perhaps—Joseph would weaken?"

"No. It's been almost a year since we met. I'm no closer to winning him today than I was the day Jonathan introduced me to him. Farther away, to put it bluntly."

"I'm sure I don't understand Joseph."

"Grace Browning says she doesn't either. They say you always want what you can't have. I've met lots of nice young men, but Joseph Harris is the only one that literally takes my breath. I suppose I'll go back to Kentucky and. . .never marry. . .and die with my dream."

At this moment, many miles to the west, Joseph and Effie pulled into the Caprock Stagestop.

Chapter 28

Joseph's Land

"*Effie!*" Grace Browning smothered her with kisses. "Our own little Effie! Joseph promised he'd bring you to see us."

"To my b-birthplace," burst Effie.

"Yes, you're a real native. Born in the Wild West!" Mrs. Browning cheered. "Did you two have a nice trip, Joseph?"

"I've never had a better traveling companion!" Joseph boasted. "And don't you tell your son-in-law I said that, either."

"I don't expect it would upset Jim," laughed Mrs. Browning. "Bring Effie's things on in. We'll put her in Charlotte's room where she'll have a magnificent western view of our country."

Joseph stepped lighter, laughed easier. Grace Browning noticed it right away and wondered. She had never seen him so happy. *Does it have anything to do with Amy?*

"How's our cousin, Amy?" Dave asked Effie at the supper table. It relieved Joseph that Effie was the one interrogated. He gave keen attention to the conversation.

"She's the best t-teacher in the w-world!" Effie was quick to respond. Grace Browning couldn't resist a sideways glance at Joseph. *Did he blush, or was it my imagination?*

"She is, eh?"

"And the p-prettiest too."

"That's because she's a Browning!"

After supper they moved to the back veranda. The sun had kindled a fiery glow in the west, then left it as a careless traveler might abandon a campfire. The twilight of the prairie patiently extinguished the last spark. Nature's drama fascinated Effie.

"The s-stars are so c-close!"

"They seem almost on top of your head, don't they?" Grace Browning agreed.

"L-like you could reach out and t-touch them."

"This is the closest place to heaven I've found, Effie," Joseph marveled at the peace he embraced tonight. "Look in that direction as far as you can see." He pointed toward the northwest. "My ranch is there. Three thousand acres of God's virgin land, complete with water and timber."

"And we can hardly wait for Joseph to get moved out here," Grace Browning told Effie. "There's nobody we'd rather have for a neighbor than Joseph Harris. That land is confirmed Harris-land."

Joseph laughed. "I thought I was the only impatient one."

Mrs. Browning brought a warm crocheted shawl and wrapped it about Effie's shoulders as the chill night air claimed the day's warmth. Effie snuggled under it, content as a purring kitten.

"I told Jim I'd try to keep the stage route alive for a year. My year is almost up. I'll turn the reins back to Jim."

"Jim won't go back on the road!" assured Mrs. Browning. "He's happy where he is—and making good money. I think he simply plans to discontinue the route—or sell it to someone else."

"Business is down to a minimum. The railroads are taking over fast."

"I-I'd like to ride a train s-sometime," Effie yawned sleepily. "And see the w-world go z-zipping by!"

"When Joseph gets moved out here, your whole family will have to come on the train to see him—and us," suggested Mrs. Browning. Effie's head began to nod.

"But right now, Grace, I think you'd better show our weary pilgrim to her resting place," Dave Browning said.

When Grace returned from tucking Effie into bed, she heard the end of Joseph's sentence: ". . .Amy's husband."

"Joseph! Don't tell me Amy got married!" she cried in dismay.

"You just heard the last of Joseph's statement, Grace," patiently explained Mr. Browning. "Joseph *thought* Amy was married all this time—to Jonathan."

"Joseph thought. . .Amy. . .married to Jonathan!" Grace Browning laughed heartily. "Whatever gave you the idea that Amy was *married,* Joseph?"

Joseph scoffed at his own foolishness. "I have a bad

habit of not paying attention, obviously. They. . .they were just together at the stage stop in Amarillo where I met them, and they were both named Browning. That's a lot of evidence, isn't it? So I assumed they were Mr. and Mrs., I guess. . . ."

So that's why Amy has been getting nowhere with Joseph Harris, concluded Mrs. Browning. *He has conscientiously kept his distance from this "married woman"!*

"Well how. . .when did you learn the difference?"

"Effie told me on this trip. To be honest, I discredited her information. I'll admit I was eager to get here to find out the truth of the matter. I knew you would know."

"I know all right. My great-uncle, Daniel Browning, only had one son, and that son had these two children, Amy and Jonathan. I can vouch for that."

"Hindsight clears up my stupid blindness," laughed Joseph. "I couldn't figure a husband leaving a young and pretty wife behind to her own devices for an indefinite time while he wandered the continent. It didn't make sense."

"I'm surprised you didn't compare eyes, noses, and hair. Why, Amy and Jonathan would pass for twins!"

"I'm afraid I didn't study *Jonathan* that closely," Joseph grinned sheepishly. "The relative they're looking for, then, is *theirs* rather than *hers* as I supposed."

"Their maternal grandparents left a large estate. There were three children in the original family. A son was killed in the Civil War. That left two daughters— Amy's and Jonathan's mother and a younger daughter who evaporated into the West. That's the one he's searching for."

"Amy says he isn't having any luck."

"I was afraid of that."

"Since. . .if they can't find this relative, what will they do?"

"Jonathan says they can go ahead and sell the estate and put the aunt's half into a trust fund in the event that any of her heirs are located in the future. It may be many years, but someone will show up eventually."

"He's gone to a lot of trouble and expense to find her, hasn't he?"

"That's Jonathan for you. He wants her to have her part. She left behind some valuable personal belongings, too. He's the administrator of the will."

"Amy said he plans to give up the search in the next few days and will be returning for her."

"They'll return to Kentucky, I suppose?"

"Unless I can prevent it." The darkness hid Joseph's blush from Grace Browning. He hurried on, "I'm anxious to talk to Jonathan about Charles and thank him for getting the land papers for me. I owe him a lot."

"Has Amy been able to help Effie? That was her purpose for accepting the teaching job, you know. . .well, one of her purposes anyway."

"Oh, yes! She's helped Effie drastically. Effie talks fifty percent better. I couldn't believe the improvement after being away during the winter months."

"You want Effie to see her mother's grave while she's here, don't you?"

"Yes, I'll take her tomorrow."

"Why don't you let me take her to tour the land and to visit the grave, Joseph?" suggested Grace Browning. "I knew Rebecca quite well, and Effie will have a lot of questions. You can help Dave here at the store. I'll enjoy the outing."

"Effie would enjoy your company," Joseph replied. "And I'm sure you could answer more of her questions than I could. I'm not even sure I could find the grave."

Daylight roused Effie gently. The clear blue sky hung just outside her window. The sun had plunged away from the shores of its horizon and begun its swim across the blue ocean of sky. She stretched lesiurely, enjoying deep breaths of the light air before getting up to dress. It was a perfect day.

After breakfast, Mr. Browning hitched the horses to the wagon for his wife and Effie. "Grace is a pretty good driver," he told Effie, "as women drivers go."

How can skin and sinew contain such excitement, Effie wondered. "I-I love it!" she crooned as Mrs. Browning took her to the small abandoned cabin nestled in the canyon, the trickling spring, and her mother's grave. The patches of blossoming cacti, scrubby mesquite and purple sagebrush pulled Effie back across the years into Rebecca's beloved world.

"W-what was my m-mother like?"

"She was as pretty as a picture, and she sparkled with happiness. I've never seen a woman love a man as she loved your father. She practically worshiped him! Like Dave always said, she was perfectly content with her land, her man, and her baby. And she loved the beauties of nature. Land! How she loved sunrises and sunsets! 'Come here, Charles, and watch God do up a morning,' she'd laugh. 'See Him pushing the sun up over the horizon?' She never once got homesick for the life she left behind, which must have been plush. She'd get a letter now and then from her folks begging her to come back home, but she told me this was now her home and she had no plans of returning to the land she came from. Then when you were a very small baby, she got word that both her mother and father had died in a malaria epidemic. She grieved for them after a natural fashion, but nothing could daunt her spirits for long."

"She died s-suddenly?"

"Sort of. She'd been going downhill and had developed a hacking cough. None of us considered it fatal, though. I sent some cough syrup and a tonic. I kept meaning to ride out to see about her, but kept putting it off. Then one day your father came in from clearing some land and found her dead. We suspected pneumonia, but without a doctor out here we had no way of knowing. Her death very nearly finished your father. I've never seen a man so unraveled by anything. I tried to get him to stay and try to adjust, but he left for Texas with you immediately, as if fleeing an invisible ghost."

Effie touched the crude headstone hewn roughly by her own father's hands. "F-father's joined her now, you know."

"Yes, Joseph told us. I'm sorry to hear it."

Effie looked long at the grave as if to seal it in her memory, then gazed away into the distance. "God t-took this sweet m-mother, but He's given me a-another just as s-sweet."

Chapter 29

The Telegram

*T*he reins of Joseph's emotions pulled toward Texas and Amy as he headed the coach westward to Santa Fe. He thought of a sermon Pastor Stevens had preached about the dangers of putting one's hands to the plow and looking back. Effie had her heart set on meeting Charlotte, and Joseph could not bear to disappoint her.

"I may decide to cut our visit with Jim and Charlotte short and get you back to school earlier, Effie."

"Th-there's no hurry. Miss A-amy said I was a-ahead anyhow."

"Do you know exactly when school will dismiss for summer?"

"May twentieth."

"You don't think Miss Amy would close school a couple of weeks early if Jonathan came for her, do you?" The painful thought had just occurred to Joseph, chafing his peace of mind.

"She said she m-might if Brother S-Stevens and the s-school board approved."

Joseph felt cold panic seize him. *What if Amy—the only girl I could ever love—got away from me now?* A sickness in the pit of his stomach sent a tightness to his chest.

"Maybe we should be going east instead of west." He slowed the horses, preparing to turn around. "I just feel like. . . ."

"D-don't worry. D-Dessie'll get my report c-card for me if M-Miss Amy has to leave before we get back. I've a-already passed to the next grade."

"But you'd want to be there to tell Miss Amy good-bye."

"But J-Joseph, I want to see Jim and C-Charlotte— and Santa Fe. We're s-so close and I might not e-ever get back this c-close again." Effie was near tears.

Against his inner urgings, Joseph continued west-ward, thoughts of Amy possessing his mind. He even ven-tured a feeble heart-prayer that Amy would not take her leave until he could return to talk with her.

When the Sangre de Cristo Mountains came into view, Effie squealed with delight. A rebellious cap of snow clung to the top of the highest peak, refusing to admit spring's advent. "I've n-never seen anything so h-heavenly!" gasped Effie. "Oh, Joseph, thank you for b-bringing me!" But even her delight did not compensate for his suffering.

Charlotte, deprived of a sibling all her life, adopted Effie, and the two enjoyed mutual fellowship while Jim and Joseph passed the lagging time in conversation. Jim felt the backwash of Joseph's emotional turbulence. He wondered what was disturbing Joseph.

"You say you're ready to throw down the reins and. . ." Jim began.

". . .get married!" cut in Joseph, laughing.

Jim jumped to the edge of his chair. "Joseph Harris, did I hear you correctly?"

"You heard me right and that's my wish," Joseph enjoyed Jim's consternation. "I'll have to consult the lady first, of course."

"You're not serious, I'm sure. You can't be. You're April foolin' me and it's almost May."

"No April fool. I'm dead serious."

"Joseph, it's not like you to be impulsive."

Joseph threw back his head in convulsive laughter. "Those are the *exact* words I said about you this time last year!"

"But. . . ."

"Jim, when you find what you've been looking for all your life, is there any reason to sit and let it slip through your fingers? Now is there?"

"I'm almost convinced you're not pulling my leg."

"I'm not."

"Well, out with it. Who is she?"

"Effie's schoolteacher."

"Not the married woman you told us about when you were here before? The wife of Charlotte's cousin, Jonathan?"

"Yes."

"Did Jonathan get killed in California or something?"

"No. I just learned that Jonathan is Amy's brother, not her husband."

241

"Joseph, how did you get it so mixed up?"

"Jumped to conclusions. No one should know better than you how good I am at that. . .like you and Lilly getting married. Remember?"

Jim slapped his knee in merriment. "Joseph, if you don't start being more *observant*. . ."

"Really. Jonathan and Amy would pass for twins. I should have seen the favor—skin coloring, eyes. . . .But it was Amy I was looking at, not Jonathan!"

"So you're madly in love with Charlotte's cousin!"

"That's putting it mildly. For lack of a better word, yes, madly. And I'll be deliriously happy if. . .if she'll have me. I'd be on my way back to Brazos Point to see that lovely schoolteacher this very minute if it wasn't for a promise I made Effie to bring her to see Charlotte."

"She'll have you, Joseph! I've never seen a woman that wouldn't knock herself out for you."

"How was it you said it? 'Thanks, buddy. I've never heard sweeter words in my life.'"

"Coach driving is over?"

"It's over. I'll take Effie home and return the coach to you on the next trip out."

"No rush. I won't be driving."

"I have the fencing bought for my ranch at Caprock. I hope I can persuade Amy to be a rancher's wife!"

"Does anyone know your plans?"

"Not even Amy. You're the only one. The Brownings have a strong suspicion, I'm sure."

Joseph paced the floor hour after hour, impatient to be on his way, but Charlotte chided, "Not until I get Effie's dress finished, Joseph."

Has any seamstress made a garment slower? Joseph

242

fretted.

Effie relished every brief hour with Charlotte. She watched with avid interest as Charlotte's feet pushed the treadle of the sewing machine forward and backward, the leather pulley turning the wheel that plunged the needle up and down to make dainty stitches on the fabric. The soft blue dress with full-tiered skirt and white collar and cuffs took shape before Effie's fascinated eyes. "I-I love it!" she chirped.

"Why is Joseph so itchy to be gone?" Charlotte asked Jim in the privacy of their room. "I've never seen him so. . .so restless."

"Joseph has a secret, Charlotte."

"Jim! Is Joseph engaged to be married? Is he in love at last?"

"Well, no. . .yes. . .not exactly. . .yes."

"You're not making sense, Jim!"

"He hasn't asked her yet, Charlotte."

"Her? Who is *her?* Are you bound to secrecy?"

"No. I mean, I don't know. I mean, I don't guess I am."

"Then who is she?"

"Your cousin."

"What cousin?"

"Amy."

"But I thought Amy was married to my cousin, Jonathan. Now I'm confused. Is this the same Amy that stayed a few days with Mother last year? Joseph said Amy was my cousin's. . . ."

"Amy is Jonathan's sister, not his wife."

"Sister?"

"Joseph just found out on this trip, and he's afraid

she's going to get away before he can get back to Texas and stop her.''

"Get away?"

"Yes. She's teaching school in his home community and when school is out, she plans to return to Kentucky."

"Oh, dear! Then I'll *hurry* and finish Effie's dress. We don't want any girl that can turn Joseph's head to get away. Especially a cousin of mine!"

Lilly's good food, Jim's mandolin playing, Effie's obvious delight in Charlotte's company, and the nightly singing around Charlotte's new piano were but obstacles in Joseph's path. He ate little and slept little, aware that time was running out for him. The magnet of his love for Amy pulled mercilessly toward the rising sun.

When at last he headed east again, calling goodbyes with abrupt haste, it was hard to keep the horses at a trot and not give them their heads for a fast run in the cool highlands. Had he been alone, he would have let them go and suffered the bouncing and jostling, but he couldn't chance injuring Effie. The two weeks between him and Brazos Point seemed like two years—an eternity. If Effie's frail body could endure the long hours, he would drive from dawn to twilight.

"I've n-never had so much f-fun in all my l-life!" Effie smiled up at Joseph, but he merely nodded, pressing grimly on.

"A-are you w-worried about s-something, Joseph?"

"I suppose I am, Effie."

"W-what?"

"I'm afraid Amy will be gone when we get home."

"We can't make it by the t-twentieth?"

"I'm afraid not."

"D-does it matter s-so much? I'm s-sure I passed."

"It matters very much, Effie. In fact, it means all the world to me to see her again."

"S-she'll be glad to see y-you. . .if s-she's still there."

"You're sure of that?"

"I'm s-sure."

Joseph meant to make only a brief stop at Caprock to water the horses and then forge on. But when Mrs. Browning met him at the door, he knew something was dreadfully wrong. Her face mirrored her worry.

"You have a telegram, Joseph. Came to Amarillo by wire and then here by express."

Joseph hurriedly hitched the animals to the hitching post in front of the inn and lifted Effie from the coach. *A telegram? What has happened?*

With shaking hands, he ripped open the envelope. *"Come at once. Stop. Mama at death's door. Stop. Matthew."*

He sat down abruptly, turning white. "W-what's wrong, Joseph?" Effie pressed.

"Mama's bad sick. Near death."

"Oh, J-Joseph." Effie began to cry and Mrs. Browning came to console her. "I s-shouldn't have insisted on g-going on to C-Caprock. I s-should have let you go h-home like you w-wanted to. I was s-selfish!"

"Effie, you had no way of knowing this would happen. I don't want you blaming yourself."

"No, honey," soothed Grace Browning. "It would have happened wherever you were."

"It's so *far* home," mourned Joseph aloud. "She could be gone by the time we get there."

"You must forget the coach and take the train,

Joseph," urged Grace Browning. "The coach is too slow. Dave will take you and Effie to Amarillo to the rail and you can be home in two days."

"That would be the wise thing to do, wouldn't it?"

"Send a telegraph in Amarillo for Matthew to meet you in The Springs."

"I w-wanted to ride a train, but not like th-this," sobbed Effie. She flung herself into Grace Browning's arms. "Oh, Mrs. Browning, p-please pray. I-I just can't l-lose *another* m-mother!"

Chapter 30

Dashed Dreams

*T*he iron monster seethed impatiently, spitting fire and smoke in dragon-like fury.

With Effie at his side, Joseph boarded the train and seated himself in the stagecoach's archenemy, painfully aware of his idle hands, bereft of reins. The locomotive puffed and growled out of the Amarillo station. The absence of straining horses, clattering hooves and the high, open view from the driver's box transported him into a new world—a world closed in with metal and glass.

Changing eras brought a nostalgic sadness, but just for today, he would gladly cast his vote with this conveyance of metallic cars along a trail of steel rails. He blessed the speeding wheels. *Anything to get me to my mother's side faster!*

"I-I'm so tired," whispered Effie. Scarcely had they lost sight of the Amarillo terminal when Joseph felt her

247

head fall gently against his arm. A merciful sleep had claimed her exhausted mind and body.

Outside the curtained windows the long span of flat land slid down the rock and knotted into loops of unexpected little hills that eventually took on trees, growing taller with the miles. The trip passed in a blur of sorrow. It seemed to Joseph that Effie, who yearned to see the world go zipping by, slept most of the way.

Matthew met them Wednesday at the depot at journey's end in Pastor Steven's gig.

"What happened to Mother, Matthew?" Joseph wasted no time in questioning his brother. "She seemed all right when Effie and I left the first of April."

"We don't know what happened. That's what makes it so bad."

"What does the doctor say?"

"He says it's apoplexy. Doesn't know what caused it. Some survive, some don't."

"Does she know. . .recognize. . .anyone?"

"No one. Not even Papa."

"How long ago did it. . .happen?"

"A week ago today. Dessie found her passed out in the floor when she came home from school."

"School is still going then?" Joseph had to know.

"Dismisses for the year Friday."

Two more days. Had we come by coach I would have missed her! "Miss Amy's brother is here already?"

"Yes, he came in by train last weekend. I sure do like him. He's a man like you'd expect Miss Amy to have for a brother."

"Yes, he's a likeable fellow. Didn't find the relative he went searching for?"

248

"Not a trace. And he's disappointed."

"I'm sure."

"He need have no regrets, though. He gave it his best shot."

"How's Papa taking the. . .shock?"

"Grieving himself sick."

"Who's been taking care of the family?"

"Sarah. She and Hank have been staying in Effie's room."

"G-good," said Effie.

"Miss Amy has been bringing in a lot of cooked food. The neighbors have been wonderful. I took off from college this week to help any way that I can. Papa will sure be glad to see you and Effie."

A tomblike silence met Joseph and Effie at the front door. The doctor had come and gone, shaking his head doubtfully. "There's nothing we can do but pray," he had told the anxious family. "And hope. . .and wait. . . ."

Joseph and Effie hurried to Martha's side. She looked ghastly, lying still and inert. Effie reached for her limp hand and stroked it lovingly. Straightening her crooked back resolutely, she looked at Joseph with a death-defying determination. "She's not g-going to d-die," she said doggedly. "She's my m-mother and I won't *let* her d-die!" Joseph turned away to hide his bitter tears, wrestling with a new truth. *If anything happens to Mother, Effie will go, too.*

He found Henry in the cow lot, milking the cow with stiff, inept hands. Milking had been Martha's chore. "Papa, what happened?"

"She just went out like a lamp, Joseph. It was worry. You know how women are about worryin'—Martha, anyhow. She just worried herself right into a stroke."

"The drought, Papa? Was she running short on food for the family?"

"She hoped on this year's garden an' crops. When th' garden burned up an' th' crops came up slow an' stunted, she went under."

"But, Papa, I don't understand. As long as you have food and raiment and a roof over your heads. . . ."

"That's th' problem, Joseph. She didn't want me to tell you, but I had to mortgage th' land and th' roof over our heads for food when we didn't make no crops ner garden last year."

"Still, it's not. . . ."

"Th' bank would only loan for one year. Th' note's due in two months an' we don't have enough to pay th' interest, much less th' principle. She couldn't stand th' thought of losin' th' place. This is home—where she raised her babies an' all. It means more to a woman than it does to a man, Joseph."

"But surely you could get an extension. There'll be some way. . . ."

"I did th' best I knowed how to do with my limited intelligence an' education, son. A man just gets broke down sometimes on life's road. Wheels fall out from under him. I borrowed th' money on th' place to keep us from starvin'. Before God, that's all I knowed to do. Th' bank don't allow no extensions. Times is hard."

"If you and Mother would have told me, Papa. . . ."

"Martha didn't want to bother your life—nor Matthew's. You'd already done more than your share, buildin' th' room for Effie an' all. She thought you should be plannin' again' yer own wife-takin'. I thought sure th' drought would bust up 'fore now an' we could pay back th' loan. But it ain't. It shore ain't."

"How much is the loan, Papa?"

"Six hundred, plus thirty dollars interest."

Joseph groaned. "If I had only known, I would not have invested my money. It took all I had saved up to transfer Charles's land into my name and buy the fencing materials. But that could have waited."

Henry stopped milking and buried his head in his hands, oblivious to the swishing of Bossy's tail in his face. "I know th' Good Lord is goin' to make a way somehow, Joseph. I put Him first, even with th' borrowed money. He ain't never let us down. That's what I kept tellin' Martha, but she didn't see no possible way to save th' place. Pastor Stevens preached a sermon on miracles. He said th' first thing God needed to perform a miracle was an impossible situation. Well, I tell you, Joseph, He's got His makin's right here for a miracle. I never seen nuthin' much more impossible! Just wish I had a little more faith."

"The doctor doesn't give any hope for Mother's recovery?"

"He said she needs to be in a good hospital. But it's sixty miles to the closest hospital an' we don't have th' money to get her admitted even if'n we could find a way to get her there."

"I'll go talk to the banker myself next week, Papa. I'll. . .I'll sell my land cheap and we'll. . .we'll keep the home place. When it's advertised that my land has plenty of good water and timber, it'll go fast." It was Joseph's hardest—and most sacrificial—decision. "You say we have two months?"

"About two months, son."

251

"That's plenty of time."

Joseph's future fell apart before his unbelieving eyes. Now he had nothing to offer Amy. Even if he dared to share his hope with her for their future together, the wait would be indefinite. *But could a responsible eldest son do less for his destitute family?*

Joseph carried the milk pail to the house for Henry. In the kitchen, Sarah busied herself with supper. The household moved mechanically, dazed with sorrow. "Mama asleep," whined Sally, leaning her curly head against Joseph's knee. "She go night-night." Joseph used his shirt sleeve to brush away his tears.

Effie had not left Martha's side. She caressed her hand, constantly talking to her, praying for her. Socks, the woolly gray cat, shared her lonely vigil.

Home in time, Joseph thought. *Amy's still here and Mother's alive. If I can only keep Amy here!*

The doctor came again before sundown. He took his stethoscope from his black bag, checked Martha's vital signs, lifted her eyelids and looked into her unseeing eyes. "No change," he proclaimed. "Her chances of complete recovery are better if she regains consciousness in the immediate future. The longer the coma persists, the more permanent disability you can expect. Keep spoon-feeding her liquids and broth. She could wake up tomorrow. She could pass on tonight. Don't get your hopes up. She is in serious condition. I'll check back periodically."

Effie looked squarely at the physician. "Th-this is my m-mother and she can't die!" she said testily. "I-I won't *let* her die! She t-took care of m-me, and now I'll take care of h-her!"

"That's the spirit, little lady!" the doctor patted Effie's head. "I've seen that kind of spunk scare the death angel away."

Effie could not be pried from Martha's side to go to school the next day. "Are you goin' to school to get your promotion card, Effie?" Dessie asked.

"N-no."

"I'll go to school for Effie's report." Joseph found the opportunity he sought. The anticipation of seeing Amy made his throat dry. He had planned his approach, hugging the happy thoughts to his bosom. Now he had nothing to offer.

"I can bring her promotion card, Joseph," Dessie offered.

"I need to talk to Miss Amy anyhow," Joseph insisted.

"About Effie?"

"About several things."

Chapter 31

Elusive Heir

Joseph timed his visit to correspond with school's dismissal. Clouds banked in the southwest, and a faint smell of rain filled the air. The bluebonnets had gone to seed, but the hollyhocks bravely fought to bring cheer against the blanched roadside. Joseph stooped to pick a bouquet of the wild beauties for Amy.

"Mr. Harris!" Amy greeted, prim and proper in her navy blue linen suit with white collar. Lights danced in her violet eyes, her joy at seeing him evident.

"Please call me Joseph." He handed her the flowers, looking directly into those violet eyes, hoping she could not hear the fierce pounding of his heart.

"Why. . .how lovely. . .Joseph!"

She had seen that gleam in his eyes once before, the day they first met and their hearts communed at the Amarillo stage stop. Her knees weakened and threatened to betray her, so she sat down quickly.

"Won't you have a chair, Joseph?" Her cheeks prepared themselves for the delightful dimples that set his heart a-flutter. "How was your trip west?"

"Too good to be true, except for the message of Mother's illness."

"I'm sorry about your mother. . .If there's anything I can do. . . ." Amy held her flowers with care, their untamed fragrance thrilling her senses. "How was my cousin Grace?"

"In perfect health and she sends you her greetings."

"And Effie. . . ?"

"She'd pass for a veteran traveler. Now however. . . she's taking Mother's illness pretty hard. . .we can't coax her from her bedside."

"May I come and see if I can comfort her?"

"Miss Browning, I. . . ." Joseph rushed to expose his purpose here, his heart goading him on.

"Please call me Amy."

"Thank you. Amy, I don't know how to begin. I have just learned on this trip that you are single. That's what made my trip so. . .special."

"What do you mean, Joseph? I've always been single."

Joseph laughed. "I have just come to that pleasant knowledge, though."

"You thought. . . ." Her dark eyes widened, making her the loveliest creature Joseph had ever seen. "You thought I was *married?*"

"Yes," Joseph answered. "As ridiculous as it seems now, I thought that Jonathan was your *husband.*"

Amy surpressed a burst of laughter, and mirth

cavorted in her eyes. "I. . .whatever led you to believe that, Joseph?" He loved the way she said his name with a special intonation. "When I first came, Pastor Stevens thought the same thing!"

"I'm afraid I'm the one who led him to believe you were married. I. . .don't know how it happened, really. But I'm happy to find that Jonathan is your brother instead." Joseph allowed his eyes to feast freely on her becoming face.

Amy blushed a rosy pink. "I. . .I'm happy you found out, too. Who set the record straight. . .for me?" Her warmth thawed his icy fears and he began to relax.

"I argued with Effie most of the way to Caprock that you were married and that she was mistaken about Jonathan being your brother. I wanted to believe her, Amy, but I dared not play games with my heart. I. . .the first time I met you. . .at the Amarillo stop. . .I loved you. But then Jonathan walked up with that cup of water and I. . .decided you belonged to him. For almost a year now I have been trying to put you out of my heart. It. . .wasn't easy. Then when I got to Caprock, I asked Dave Browning about you and he confirmed Effie's report that you and Jonathan were indeed brother and sister, his second cousins. In the mouth of two or three witnesses. . . ."

So that's why Joseph put a padlock on his heart. She loved him the more for it. Amy laughed a pure, full laugh, threaded with the ripple he remembered shrinking from. Now he was enraptured by the sound of it. "Thank God for witnesses!"

"Thus convinced that you were. . .perhaps available . . .it was hard not to start home that night. . .for fear you would be gone back to Kentucky when I arrived. Had not the telegram reached us and we took the train home, I'm afraid I would have missed you. Behind every storm cloud is a silver lining."

"I had planned. . .that is, I plan to go this weekend, tomorrow being the final day of school this year."

"You have made plans to return next year?"

"I have turned in my resignation. I. . .won't be teaching next year."

"I. . .there were some things I wanted to discuss—some plans I had for me and you, but Mother's illness has caused me some reverses that have destroyed those plans."

"Did you get everything worked out with the land papers that Jonathan sent to you?"

"Beautifully! I got my ranch and I bought materials to start working it right away, but I'm afraid I'll have to give up my dreams now."

"Joseph. . .why?"

"To help my family here. They are in a terrible financial strait and are in danger of losing the home place. The worry of it put Mother where she is today. I'll have to forfeit my land—sell it—to get them out of. . .out of debt. In a few weeks, they'll lose everything they've worked a lifetime for if I don't. I'll have to act fast."

"I. . .I understand." Her eyes went tender, filled with genuine compassion. "You're a good. . .son."

"I see no other solution. I'll see what I can work out with the bank and I'll. . .I'll talk to you again before you. . .leave."

"Jonathan wants to talk with you about your uncle and I want to see. . .Effie. May. . .may we come over tonight, Joseph?"

"Please do, Amy. I'd. . .we'd all be delighted. . .and comforted." Joseph's heart was in his eyes and Amy, with schoolteacher perception, read him like a book. The wall of resistance was gone. *Oh, joy! Mrs. Stevens will never believe this. . .or Pauline. . .or Grace Browning. . .or Jonathan.* Amy found it hard to believe herself. The teaching job had paid big dividends.

Joseph helped Sarah clean up the table after supper. "Amy and Jonathan are coming tonight," he told her, a cheery note in his voice that she hadn't heard for months. "Jonathan has some information to share with me about Uncle Charles." Joseph shaved and changed into his best clothes.

When Jonathan and Amy arrived, it pleased Joseph to note that Amy was not embarrassed at the family's shabby dwelling. After paying a visit to Martha's room, she made herself right at home, taking Sally onto her lap for a hug.

Henry brought chairs into the sitting room for everyone, and Jonathan launched into a description of his travels. "I believe God directed me to Mrs. Bimski's boarding house," he said. "It was while I was searching through the registers that I found the name of Charles Harris in the December, 1878, journal. His home address was listed as Caprock, Territory of New Mexico, and I knew I had found your brother, Mr. Harris."

"It couldn't have been no coincident," Henry agreed. "I don't believe in coincidents."

"I went to Mrs. Bimski who has a marvelous memory and asked her all about Charles. As it turned out, he had been one of her favorite tenants."

"Everybody loved my brother," Henry inserted. "He

had a big heart an' a winnin' way."

"She said he had worked hard and was making plans to return to the child he left with relatives in Texas when he was shot and killed. She feels sure he was mistaken for someone else. She said she never knew of an enemy."

"He wrote us a letter that he planned to return in a fortnight," Henry said. "That's the last we heard."

"They never learned where he had his gold stored—and probably never will—but he had left the papers I sent Amy in his room—his marriage license and the land documents. I didn't look at them."

"He's buried there?" Joseph asked.

"Mrs. Bimski laid him to rest in the city cemetery, a beautiful vine-enclosed park in Los Angeles. She cried because she didn't have the address of a relative to notify of his demise. Her minister performed the duties, and a host of his friends from the hotel followed the bier. They gave him a proper burial."

"I'm glad he had friends."

"Mrs. Bimski said he was never without friends. An oldtimer at the lodge told me the young ladies tried to attract his attention, but he told Mrs. Bimski that after knowing a lady like his Rebecca, no one else could ever replace her. He talked of her and Effie incessantly."

"Yes, according to the Brownings, Charles and Rebecca were very much in love." Joseph found Amy's eyes and held them.

"The headstone is simple, but most impressive. It gives the date of his birth and the date of death and has an inscription that reads: 'To live in the lives of those we leave behind is not to die.' "

Henry wiped his eyes on a soiled handkerchief. "It

comforts my heart to know that my brother had a decent, Christian burial. An' what a beautiful sayin' on th' marker. I'll write th' lady a note of thanks an', when we're able, we'll repay her ever' penny for th' funeral expenses."

"She won't hear of it. I offered to pay her back myself, and she scorned my offer. She said if it had been one of her own in a distant land, she would have been glad for someone to do the same for her. She said the Lord had rewarded her a hundredfold."

"I'm beholdin' to 'er."

"She said she'd be glad to put you up in a nice room free of charge in Charles's memory if you could ever make the trip out to visit his grave for yourself."

"We're beholdin' to you, too, Jonathan."

"I feel that my trip was well rewarded by finding this information about Charles even though I didn't find our own lost loved one."

"You have given up entirely on your aunt?" Joseph asked.

"I went over the entire state with a fine-tooth comb," Jonathan said. "I put ads in all the papers, and ran her picture, too. I'm convinced she's not there. Never been there."

Chapter 32

The Finale

"*M*iss Amy!" Effie heard her teacher's voice and made her way to Amy's side. "J-Joseph was a-afraid you'd be gone!"

"I was getting worried myself!" Amy smiled. "I couldn't bear the thoughts of not seeing you. . .and Joseph. . .before I left."

"You're n-not leaving soon, I h-hope?"

"I'm not. . .sure."

"J-Joseph thought you were *m-married!*"

"That's what he told me. Thank you for setting the record straight for me."

"I t-thought he'd never b-believe me! T-that's why he wouldn't let you be his s-sweetheart."

"That makes me more proud of him than ever, Effie. But things will be different now. . .I'm sure."

"I'm s-sorry Jonathan didn't f-find your a-aunt."

"I am too, Effie. She left so many nice things behind that I don't know what to do with—a whole room of lovely furniture, pretty clothes, a cedar chest filled with keepsakes. It seems a shame to sell her personal items to a stranger."

"Y-yes. Her c-children would want them."

"That's what I thought. And that's why Jonathan searched so long. A few of the things I might be able to store, but the homeplace Mother and Father left us is already furnished and we'd like to keep our own furnishings."

"Of c-course. Do you r-remember your aunt?"

"Not much. I was only four years old when she left for the frontier. According to her picture, she was a beautiful lady."

"L-like you!"

Amy gave a subdued laugh. "Jonathan says we favor, but she was much prettier than I!"

"P-pictures are nice. I h-have one of my own m-mother when she was a g-girl."

"And you got to visit your birthplace and your mother's grave?" Amy led on, sensing the need to draw Effie's mind away from her obsession with Martha for a time of mental rest.

"Yes, M-Miss Amy. Isn't C-caprock a w-wonderful place? Th-the stars are so close you can most n-nigh touch them. I l-love the Brownings and C-Charlotte."

"Yes. I love Caprock. It would be nice to live there."

"D-do you know C-Charlotte?"

"I didn't get to meet Charlotte, but I'm anxious to."

"She's s-sweet. She m-made me a new dress."

"Did Joseph take you on a tour of his ranch land?"

"Mrs. B-Browning did. And she t-told me all about my m-mother. M-mother loved s-sunrises and s-sunsets and r-rainbows and b-butterflies. She liked to w-watch God m-make a m-morning, and h-hang the c-colored curtains in the sky in the e-evening! M-maybe she just l-loved His h-handiwork so much that He d-decided to take her to h-heaven where she could see it a-all!"

"That's probably just what He decided."

"W-would you like to see a p-picture of my m-mother?"

"Why sure, Effie!"

Effie went for Rebecca's Bible. "Th-this was her B-Bible," she explained. "She had all her f-favorite scriptures m-marked and most of them were about h-heaven. I like this one b-best in J-John. 'In my F-Father's house are many mansions. . . .' That means a real p-pretty house. Our family records are h-here, too. And my b-birthdate."

"I think that's perfectly lovely!"

"I k-keep her picture in the f-front of the B-Bible. That's where it was w-when my d-daddy brought me here." She sat down beside Amy with the Book on her lap, holding it reverently.

"M-Mother was very p-pretty. Like y-you!"

"Why, thank you, Effie!"

Effie fumbled with the cover of the Bible and handed the portrait to Amy. "S-see!"

Amy took the portrait and gave a startled cry. "Jonathan!" Both he and Joseph ran to her side.

"What's the matter, Amy? You're as pale as death! Are you ill?"

"The *picture!*" She shoved it toward Jonathan.

"It's. . .it's *Aunt Annie!* Look! It's just like the one we have, only a different pose!"

Jonathan read the inscription written beneath the likeness in neat calligraphy. *Rebecca Ann Franklin.* "Amy! This is our own aunt! Where? . . .Who. . . ? Where did you find this picture?"

"Effie says it's her *mother!* If that is so, then Effie is Aunt Annie's own child!"

"But Amy, that is impossible. Aunt Ann married a man named Andrews."

"H-here." Effie opened the Bible to the family records in the center.

Jonathan stared in disbelief. He read, *Rebecca Ann Franklin and Charles Andrew Harris were united in Holy Matrimony on the 23rd day of July, the year of our Lord Eighteen Hundred and Seventy-Two by Rev. W. D. Hollingsworth.* "Our own Brother Hollingsworth, Amy!"

"Andrew was her husband's *middle* name instead of his last name."

"Nina called him Charles Andrew. I thought Andrews was his surname!"

"No wonder I couldn't find Ann Andrews. It was Rebecca Ann *Harris!* The search is over, and I visited my own uncle's grave!"

"See here. Mother and Grandmother and Grandfather were witnesses to the marriage. *Mrs. Mary Elizabeth Franklin Browning and Mr. and Mrs. R. L. Franklin,"* Amy pointed out. "And here's Uncle Johnathan for whom you were named. . .our uncle that was killed in the war. Only he spelled his name differently."

"And here are Effie's credentials, Amy. *Effie Rebecca Harris was born to Rebecca Ann and Charles Andrew*

266

Harris on April 24, 1875."

Joseph studied the photo, then looked at Amy. That's where he had seen those eyes before. Amy had inherited Rebecca Harris's beautiful violet eyes!

"Effie!" Amy wrapped her arms around her favorite pupil. "You're my very own first cousin. And you're the heir we're looking for. The *only* heir. What if I had never come to Brazos Point to teach?"

"We have a buyer for our Grandfather Franklin's estate, Effie," Jonathan explained to the newly found heiress. "I'm holding out for fifty thousand dollars. And we'll get it. Half of it will be yours."

"And all your mother's lovely furniture falls to you, Effie," Amy reminded.

"Is th-there any m-money right n-now?"

"Yes, there's the lease money for this past year. It's in the bank. I can write you a check for your part now if you need it."

"H-how much?"

"Six hundred dollars plus accrued interest of five percent."

"To F-father. For the m-mortgage."

Now how did Effie know about the debt, wondered Henry. *You could never hide anything from the bent-winged angel.*

"Is it e-enough, F-father?"

Exactly."

"There's your miracle, Papa," Joseph smiled.

"I can bring a check tomorrow," Jonathan offered. "It'll be my happy privilege, in fact."

Amy caught Joseph's eye. "You get to keep your land!" she whispered.

"*Our* land," he smiled into Amy's eyes. . .Rebecca's eyes. It was his marriage proposal—uniquely Joseph.

Only Effie heard, and when they looked around she had left the room. Amy and Joseph found her, but were held spellbound just outside the door of Martha's room by the invisible barrier of something too sacred for interruption—the crooning voice of Effie pouring out her love to Martha.

"S-sweet mother. E-everything will be all right n-now. The mortgage d-debt is all p-paid and we won't lose our h-home. Can you hear m-me, sweet m-mother? Grandfather F-Franklin left me some m-money." She kissed Martha's hand and softly brushed her face.

"If y-you'll just w-wake up, we'll build you a nice b-big house. You can have the w-warming oven you wanted and an inside l-lavatory with a c-cast iron bathtub and a w-washing machine with a w-wringer so you won't have to w-work so hard.

"Joseph's g-going to marry Miss A-Amy and you have to w-wake up and see the b-beautiful wedding. They're so in l-love!

"Wake up, s-sweet mother. Everything's p-paid. Can you hear m-me? It's all c-clear. M-mother?"

Martha stirred restlessly. Effie tugged insistently at her hand. "Y-you'll walk again, M-mother! Y-you'll talk again! You'll be all w-well!"

Slowly Martha opened her eyes and smiled wanly at Effie. Joseph's arm encircled Amy as she laid her head on his broad shoulder and wept for joy.

"We'll h-have plenty of m-money now, sweet m-mother. Don't worry about a-anything."

Martha's words were intelligible. "S-sweet daughter," she whispered thickly. "Th-thank you!"

LAJOYCE MARTIN, a minister's wife, has written for Word Aflame Publications for many years with numerous stories and books in print. She is in much demand for speaking at seminars, banquets, and camps. Her writings have touched people young and old alike all over the world.

OTHER BOOKS *by LaJoyce Martin*

The Harris Family Saga:
To Love a Bent-Winged Angel
Love's Mended Wings
Love's Golden Wings
When Love Filled the Gap
To Love a Runaway
A Single Worry
Two Scars Against One
The Fiddler's Song
The Artist's Quest
To Say Goodbye

Pioneer Romance:
Brother Harry and the Hobo
Destiny's Winding Road
Heart-Shaped Pieces
Light in the Evening Time
Love's Velvet Chains
Mister B's Land
The Wooden Heart
To Strike a Match

Historical Romance:
So Swift the Storm
So Long the Night

Historical Novel:
Thread's End

Western:
The Other Side of Jordan
To Even the Score

Path of Promise:
The Broken Bow
Ordered Steps

Children's Short Stories:
Batteries for My Flashlight

Nonfiction:
Alpha-Toons
And They All Lived Happily Ever After
Coriander Seed and Honey
Heroes, Sheroes, and a Few Zeroes
I'm Coming Apart, Lord!
Mother Eve's Garden Club

Order from:
Pentecostal Publishing House
8855 Dunn Road
Hazelwood, MO 63042-2299